Oliver Howard

ALL RIGHT GOOD NIGHT

What happened to Malaysian 370?

Cover illustration by Chandler Book Design
www.chandlerbookdesign.co.uk

Typeset in Linotype Optima®
Printed by createspace.com

Published by Oliver Howard MMXIV
v.1.0.4

ISBN 978-0-9930155-0-2

CONTENTS

PREFACE

This novel is inspired and informed by the disappearance of Malaysian Air flight 370 in March 2014. Along with the rest of the world, the author watched in horror and disbelief as the tragedy unfolded and information was withheld, released, retracted and corrected in a confusing and frustrating torrent of events.

A picture eventually emerged which to someone with an inside knowledge of aviation pointed to a deliberate act. An aircraft cannot fly that far, and go through such a complex series of movements, without someone in control.

This led to the hypothesis that the world could now be facing a kind of terrorism it has never seen before. No-one claimed responsibility, but that was also the case in the New York, London and many other terrorist attacks. The question was, where is the terror in making an airliner disappear?

An idea therefore emerged that maybe this was the first action in a wider plan; that we had only seen the beginning, and from that sprang the inspiration for this novel. The author wishes to stress that this is a work of fiction and does not claim to be an accident analysis or—save for the first chapter—a representation of real events which, although they may be similar, are likely to have been completely different.

The author acknowledges and deeply respects the loss and the grief of the loved ones of everyone on board Malaysian 370 and extends his condolences to everyone so affected. It is his sincere hope that this novel does not add to the burden of this tragedy.

If anything, but this is just a dream, it might prevent a recurrence if someone in power had enough foresight and courage to take the premise of this book just a little bit seriously.

The author is a US Airline Transport Pilot with 18 years of international flying in General Aviation. He has flown in most parts of the world, including many remote regions and oceanic crossings, and has first hand experience of most of what he describes. Even so, artistic licence has been taken in the description of some situations.

The author also has a background in IT and was a co-founder of a software company at the dawn of personal computing. This experience provides inspiration and source material for the descriptions of a small group of people who in this novel are turned into terrorists by traumatic events. It is pure fabrication but serves as a conduit for the conflicts and frustrations that exist all over the world today.

The plot may seem far fetched, but so was the idea of flying airliners into skyscrapers until someone did it.

June 2014

Oliver Howard

1. THE FLIGHT

Malaysian Airlines flight 370 lifts off from Kuala Lumpur Airport eleven minutes late, at 41 minutes past midnight on March 8, 2014 on a routine night flight to Beijing. The 227 passengers and 12 crew members on board have six hours of flying ahead of them before their scheduled arrival in China's capital at 6.30 AM. Or possibly eleven minutes later, unless they can catch up on the way.

After twenty minutes' flight, at one minute past one, one of the two pilots on the aircraft reports by radio to Malaysian Air Traffic Control, call sign Lumpur Radar, that they have reached their cruising altitude of 35000 feet, or flight level 350 as it is called in aviation shorthand:

"Malaysian three seven zero, maintaining level three five zero."

Lumpur Radar acknowledges the report by reading back the aircraft's call sign:

"Malaysian three seven zero."

The pilots are following a highway in the sky called Airway R208 which is defined by a string of waypoints used for navigation and reporting. A few minutes later, they are passing over the lights of Kuala Terengganu on the east coast of Malaysia and head out over the dark waters of the South China Sea towards Vietnam in the north-east.

Nineteen minutes past one, Malaysian 370 is approaching a waypoint on their route, named IGARI, which is a few miles before the end of Malaysian airspace and the beginning of Vietnamese. Lumpur Radar radios a handover message instructing the pilots to call Vietnamese Air Traffic Control for continued services and clearances:

"Malaysian three seven zero contact Ho Chi Minh one two zero decimal nine. Good night."

One of the pilots replies:

"Good night, Malaysian three seven zero."

The textbook response would have been: "Ho Chi Minh 120 decimal 9, Malaysian 370," which includes the new radio frequency in the reply. This is usually followed by a "bye bye" or "good night," depending on the hour, to soften the precise but frosty nature of aviation English. In fact, by convention, leaving it out would be equal to slamming the door in the face of the controller. Pilots sometimes do it on purpose if a controller has been difficult or uncooperative, but in normal circumstances these little courtesies help oil the wheels of aviation's complex and delicate machinery.

But the pilot's slightly non-standard reply this night indicates nothing untoward. It is fairly typical of the relaxed nature of routine communications between pilots and air traffic controllers the world over. It is also the last communication from an entirely unremarkable flight which moments later is transformed into the deepest and darkest mystery so far in aviation history.

Two minutes on, twenty one minutes past one in the morning, the response from the aircraft's radar transponder disappears from Air Traffic Control radar. Nine minutes later, at one thirty, the last radar echo from the plane fades from the screens.

Three hundred tons of Boeing 777 jet airliner with 229 people from fourteen different nations on board, between the ages of 2 and 79, appear to have vanished from the surface of the Earth.

What follows in the coming days, weeks and months is heart-wrenching agony for the hundreds of affected families and friends of all these people.

As time drags on, confusion, contention and controversy ensue as the flight and the reasons for its disappearance are picked over ever more desperately by experts, press and politicians, not to mention social media.

Then conflicts over costs and liabilities start appearing between airlines, authorities, manufacturers and insurers, leaving the bereaved largely sidelined and abandoned.

2. THE GAME

I woke up to a grey morning with an empty feeling as if time had stopped. Then, as I lay watching the hands of my alarm clock jump past noon, I realised it wasn't morning any more, but afternoon, and that time was not standing still after all.

I felt just as dull and grey on the inside as the scene outside my fifth floor bedroom window on our South London estate. A sea of grey concrete marred by ugly, black stripes left by dirty city rain, set against an empty, grey sky. Small drops on the window showed it was raining as well. Or drizzling, rather. Not even the rain could get going properly.

It was not as if I had been boozing the night before. I had been working. Till five in the morning. It's what I did when I was on a roll. In more ways than one—when things gelled and everything came together beautifully, but also when I had anything to do at all. It was September 2006 and the world was booming, but my work still came in fits and starts. Months of nothing, then months of mad rush to finish a job someone else should have finished six months ago. That's where I was now, and I was nearing the end.

I was a freelance programmer. Yeah, that's right, a geek, a nerd, and I had the looks to go with it—skinny, pasty and even a little spotty from time to time. But it was a living, and I actually liked it. No, I loved it. To me there were few things more fulfilling in life than turning a client's abstract and muddled real-world problem into beautiful data structures and clear, consistent computer code. I was deeply happy when I saw my creations come alive, and I didn't care if people thought that was a sad, little life. It wasn't, not to me. But it was hard work sometimes.

The other side of the bed was cold and unmade. Omar, my partner, had probably been up early as usual even on a Saturday, and had left the bed like that so as not to wake me. Life started seeping back into me as I got on with my morning rituals—toothbrush, shower, coffee, a slice of toast. Oh, go on Nigel, spoon on the jam, it's not as if you're getting fat. In the end I even made the bed.

"Hello-o, anyone ho-ome?"

It always made me cringe when he did that. Put on his little girl voice. But I put on my glad face.

"Hi-i, look what I-I've got."

It was his dragging out of the vowels that did it. I didn't like it, but I knew he had a need to do it, so it was best done when we were alone.

Omar stopped dead in the doorway and looked at me.

"Hey, what's the matter with you." The voice had gone.

"Nothing. I'm fine." I tried to sound chipper, but only managed to sound like I tried.

"Oh, c'mon Nigel. You're not mad because I've been out, are you?" He didn't know, and I was glad.

"Of course not."

"Because I've been shopping, then?" He was working round to getting me into a position where his spending was my fault.

"No, no. What have you bought?"

"Just a few things. Think you'll li-ike them." The voice was back.

I'd heard him dump something in the corridor, so I knew he was only showing me the least of it. Then when the credit card statement arrived, he'd say "but I showed you that" and look hurt.

Served me right for choosing to live with a woman, I suppose. But when we met I thought he was a man. Well, dammit, you know what I mean. Gay, obviously, but still a man; that's what I had always found for myself. Two blokes together, simple and uncomplicated, in and out of bed. In and out of relationships.

But although Omar was a man from nature's hand, he was a woman on the inside. By the time I found out, it was too late; I was too deeply in love with him. Couldn't tell him about the bits of him I didn't like, would have hurt him too much. And I was afraid he'd leave me, I suppose. He was the kind of person who could just up and leave; he'd done that before; that's how he came to be here. And he satisfied something deep inside me nobody had ever done. In a way precisely because he was a man and a woman at the same time. Sometimes more one than the other, but always both.

That was both wonderful and difficult to live with, but live with it I did.

He held the bag up to my face and cracked it open just enough for me to catch a glimpse of something black, and very thin as far as I could see. I knew we'd have fun with it later and gave him a smile.

"That's better. Now tell me what's up."

"Oh, it's just my morning blues."

"Morning! It's past one."

"To me it's morning. Dunno why, but I got thinking about 9/11. Remember?"

"Remember? Of course I remember. Why, I haven't got the dust out of all my clothes yet."

*

Omar grew up in New York but moved north to get a computer degree from MIT. He had just moved back to New York for his first job when 9/11 happened. He lived three blocks from Ground Zero and told me his cereal tasted of it for months. Couldn't get it out of all the nooks and crannies of his life, so in the end he moved to California. He loved life with the laid back hippie bunch out there but also began to make a name for himself as a programmer and met some important people in the business. When the offers started to roll in, he took a job in London to see some of the world and as an intellectual challenge. He knew that some of the best people in the business were British, and Omar Farid was now one of the most sought-after computer programmers in the UK.

That's how we met. One day I walked into a meeting with a client and there he was, my golden boy. His Moroccan emigrant father and half Navajo mother had given him a stunningly beautiful, light golden skin and a finely chiselled face. I thought he was a new poster boy for their latest ad campaign and wondered what he was doing with a bunch of nerds discussing updates to the customer database software.

Even when he was introduced as the company's new head of database resources, I couldn't believe it. Nobody can look like that and be a geek. But when he opened his mouth, it took me only a few seconds to realise that this guy was no poster boy. He summed up the job in hand with a few, clear statements in his soft and measured American English, more Boston than New York, that gave away a considerable, but quiet intellect.

His voice also told me he was gay, not by anything that was there, but by the way he was trying hard to conceal it. I just had to look at the way he moved, especially his hands, to be sure. I was completely in awe, and I was also falling head over heels in love. But I didn't think I'd have a chance with someone like Omar. Take a look in the mirror, Nigel.

*

"What about 9/11? Now, I mean. That was five years ago." He raised an eyebrow as he glanced at me quizzically.

"That's just it. Five years and nothing's happened."

"What d'you mean, nothing's happened?"

"Well except for everybody forming neat lines at the airport and nobody daring to joke about Muslims, tell me what's changed. Western capitalism is still running the whole world, the same people are poor. No, the same *nations* are poor. It was just a hiccup."

"Thousands died."

"I know that. But nothing compared to the number of people who die in traffic accidents every year. Or are killed by mundane things like the measles or falling off ladders or something. In fact, I looked it up. Almost the exact same number of people die each year from *ear infections*, for chrissakes. The point is that knocking down a couple of iconic buildings and killing a few thousand people had a short term shock effect, but no real long term consequences. D'you know, the bastards just adapted to it, fucking evoluted, that's what they did. Like Darwin's turtles, they adapted to survive." I had a habit of going slightly off track when I got excited, and I sometimes lost it. But Omar was with me all the way.

"I know. What you gonna do about it?"

"Dunno. Talk about it for starters. At least with you."

"Talk away."

Then I remembered another reason I put up with his girlie stuff. The woman in him made him a tremendous listener, and maybe that's what I couldn't find in a man who was just a man, even if he was gay; a need to be listened to. Really listened to, and understood. Omar wasn't just listening idly, he understood.

The way I understood him. He said he'd never known anyone who figured him out the way I did; that's why we were together. It didn't hurt to know that he hadn't chosen me for my body; nobody ever had, well maybe except for one part of it. I wouldn't have chosen my body if I'd had the chance. But it made me feel good to know he'd chosen me for my mind. I liked my mind.

"What do they call 9/11? I mean, apart from nine-eleven."

"Bush called it Terrorism on day one."

"Precisely. And what's that?"

"Making people fear something'"

"Exactly. Making many more people than you could ever kill live in fear of being killed. But that's only the half of it. What's the point of making people fear something if it doesn't lead to anything? And it didn't. Well, not apart from a lot of hullabaloo about security and standing in lines and taking your shoes off and people can't take their toothpaste on an aeroplane any more. Big deal!"

"Why was that, d'you think?"

"I think it was because there was no follow-through. Maybe not even a plan to do a follow-through. It was like it was just a stab in the dark. And I think the West knew that. All that nonsense about a war on terror Bush talked about was just an excuse to subsidise his friends and a way to get re-elected."

"Which was one and the same."

"Yes. Bin Laden and his merry men did the bastard a favour. Like Khrushchev did for Kennedy."

"He didn't get re-elected."

"No, he got shot. But before that he got popular. And a place in history. Well, alright, he'd have got that anyway by getting himself shot, but Khrushchev made him look like a statesman. He handed him that on a silver plate."

"Krus-who?"

"My point exactly. In fifty years no-one will remember bin Laden's name but people will still remember Bush, even if they mix him up with his dad. Anyway, that's beside the point. The point is that it didn't change anything. As I said, the same people run the world and the same people are dirt poor."

"What should they have done?"

"Attacked again. Before the bastards had time to catch their breath."

"I was there, remember."

"I know. I would have found someone else."

He threw a cushion at me.

"No, but seriously. They should have thrown a second punch. What's a left hook without an uppercut?"

"Shut up. You don't know anything about boxing."

"No, but you get the picture, don't you? Why do all that when all it does is make the enemy stronger and put yourself on the run? Currencies didn't collapse, banks didn't fold, they didn't start fighting each other. That must have been what those guys were after."

"Who?"

"Bin Laden and whoever was behind him. Maybe that's what went wrong, really. Their aim was too narrow. It was religion, or religion and politics; don't think it makes much difference to those guys. But don't forget, in America money is God before God is. They didn't go for the money. Not the serious money."

"Even though they attacked the biggest fucking symbols of capitalism? The two biggest dildos in the world." Omar made eyes like teacups.

"I know. It was all symbolism. Twin Towers, Pentagon, White House. Icons of money and power. Not just in America, for the whole effing West. It wasn't just Jihadists against the West. It was all sorts of people in the West against the West around that time too. Timothy McVeigh wasn't a Jihadist. The IRA aren't exactly Muslim. Waco wasn't a Jihadist siege. The Basques aren't Islamists. I could go on."

"The IRA aren't fighting the US, they get most of their money from them."

"Don't quibble. My point is that to win a war against something as well established as Western capitalism they've got to be a lot smarter. And find ways to work together."

"Good luck getting a bunch of atheists, Protestants, Catholics and Muslims to work together."

"They'll have to think about it, though." Which reminded me of something I'd been wanting to ask him, and I wanted to change the subject anyway. I was working myself up, I could hear it. I was swearing too much; that's always a sign I should give it a rest.

"Did you think about the idea I have for a game?"

"Yes, but how's it going to work? For a start, how's it going to make any money?"

"Doesn't matter. Not to begin with. We need to get a lot of people to play it, then we'll think of something. Advertising, selling add-ons, whatever. There's still a shedload of money to be made on the internet. Not by going public now after dotcom, but by operating out there. Trick is to get a lot of users, then get a small sum off each of them."

"Well, it matters to me. I usually get paid to code," Omar said.

"I know, so do I."

"You call that code?"

I tried to look hurt. I was not in his league, but I didn't mind. He usually didn't browbeat me with it. If he was software's Shakespeare, I was a hack. His code was elegant, inspired, sometimes even divine while the best I could say about my own was that it was solid and reliable. But at least we had a common language, and most of the time we understood what the other said.

And I had the best ideas. I think he knew that even if he never said so.

"You will. Just not now. You'll get share options."

"I'll get fucking founder shares, that's what I'll get." He pretended to be fuming.

It was good natured banter, but it could be about a lot of money if we pulled it off. Omar's swearing was a sign he was getting interested.

"Of course you will," I said. After all, it was 2006 and there was only one way: up, up, up, and everybody thought it would never end. "But let's get it made first."

"No, let's agree on how to share it first. Then we can have fun making it. How do you see it?"

I had thought about some broad outlines, but no details. Not before he'd told me he was interested, so now I had to think on my feet. I knew he would need motivation, so instead of quibbling over percentages I decided to make him an offer he couldn't refuse. Half, can't say fairer than that.

"Thirty per cent each with forty percent set aside for options later."

"Why not just fifty-fifty?"

"Thought I'd make it thirty in honour of your birthday." He had a round one coming up and didn't want to talk about it, so I was teasing him with it. "No, because then we have to issue more shares if we need them for key people later on. Then we'd be diluting the existing shares, and that's a risk. Sometimes people get into fights and start diluting some shares more than others. It's a source of conflict I don't want to build in from the start." That wasn't just quick thinking; I had seen it happen.

He looked doubtful. Brilliant as he was, he found business boring, and that made him suspicious of anyone who didn't, even me.

"But you could just issue those share options to yourself."

"No I couldn't. As long as they are not issued, thirty-thirty is the same as fifty-fifty. We each have half. In fact that's not a fantastic idea either because that could put us into a deadlock. It would be better if someone had a swing vote, but I don't know who that should be."

"So half the shares each, and half the votes each?"

"Effectively, to begin with. We'll have to agree if and how to start issuing share options. They don't necessarily have to get voting rights. Depends, we'll see how it pans out. We just need to agree on something simple so we don't start fighting when it takes off."

"I agree. Let me think about it."

"Can we talk about the rest in the meantime?"

"Sure. You were talking about some kind of role-play, weren't you? Isn't that where dimwits run round the woods dressed up as Robin Hood?"

"That's just one kind, live action. Role-play started as a board game, but it's huge on-line now."

"OK, so how can we make something that's different?"

"We need to make it more attractive to more people. As it is, players select a role and play it according to a set of rules. I want people to be able to design their own roles and to some degree set their own rules. And more or less everybody should be able to interact with everybody else as long as everybody wants to."

"What, Vikings against tanks and Romans against machine guns?"

"Maybe not exactly, but in principle, yes why not? If a Roman legion thinks it can take on a machine gun position, let them do it. They may use superior tactics or maybe the Romans had a weapon we haven't heard of yet that could beat machine guns. Players should be able to invent their own weapons. But that's details. The idea is to make the whole thing more flexible, fewer rules, more fun. And the real key is that you can be whatever you want to be."

"Sounds like anarchy. Everybody will want to be generals."

"Yes it's more anarchic than all the other games. That's the whole idea, that's why people will love it. But I don't think everybody will want to be generals. Probably most people want to be heroes. Pilots and tank commanders and spies and things like that. Knights on white horses, double-oh sevens and Red Barons. Anyway, we can regulate that. Make it bloody unattractive to be anything everybody wants to be if that becomes a problem."

"So how do we get anyone to play the boring bits?"

"That's just it. We don't. Instead we provide them."

"You mean the game does?"

"Yes. We'll fill in all the spaces others don't. Who's to say if it's a real live player or one we've generated? That way we also control the whole thing as much as we want."

Omar gave me one of his looks. The one that said "Wish I'd thought of that." But he didn't bear grudges, he just quickly adopted an idea if he liked it. That was OK with me, I had plenty more.

"A heck of a lot of programming," he said.

"Yes but not as much as you think. Most games look like they are hard coded. Each character has its own code. That's why they are so one-dimensional. We should make our characters generic. Then we basically only have to program one character who can then be made to do whatever we want it to do simply by changing its parameters. You know, all a character does is move up, down, left, right, back and forth. And then they throw things at other characters—punches, stones, sticks, spears, bombs, torpedoes, rockets, nukes, whatever. They're all the same, it's just a bunch of different parameters that determine what they look like and how they behave."

"Sure. Way to go," he said in a distant voice. He was starting to take it seriously. "Could do the same with the game itself. Or games, there could be lots of different ones. There's really only one, but we can apply as many sets of rules as we want. And different worlds. That'll also make it easier for them to interact with each other."

"And the rules don't just say what a player can do. They decide what weapons and equipment they have, how it can be used, who can see and hear and do what, and who they can do it to. In fact the whole world, the whole universe of the game is just different rules for different places. The same few processes over and over again, just with different parameters."

"Brilliant." I could see he regretted it the second he said it. Omar was a sweet man, but he didn't give many compliments. At least not out of bed, but leave that to one side for now.

"That way we can spend a lot more time putting flesh on the characters and on the different games. Instead of cardboard cut-outs they'll come alive. It's a whole new ball game."

"I can see that. Not that I ever played any of them, but maybe that's because they aren't good enough. We're talking multi-player, I guess?" He raised an eyebrow.

"Of course. Multi-player, multi-role, multi-platform. We'll be the most popular game in the Universe in two years."

"Multi-platform?"

"Yes, it's got to work on anything and everything. We can start with PCs, but there's a lot of smartphones out there and many people think tablet computers are the next big thing. We have to run on anything people want to play games on."

"Tablets? Mmm. Not as simple as it sounds."

"I'm not saying we have to do it all right away, and there aren't really any tablets out there yet anyway. We'll go with the biggest platform to start with, just keep in mind it needs to be ported later on. To something we don't even know what is yet."

"Makes sense. Have you thought of a name?"

"That's the easiest part. There are thousands of war games and role-play games and stuff out there. But the one name I had thought of all the time hasn't been used by anybody."

"What's that?"

"TheWar. One word, capital W."

"Great name." High praise, for the second time in a day. No, in an hour. I was beginning to feel a need to pinch myself. Maybe I was still asleep and it was all a sweet dream.

3. THE FLIGHT DECK

Captain Agung Gupta turns slightly in his seat and looks across at his first officer. Her trim body in the crisp short-sleeved shirt merges into the gloom of the dark flight deck. But her face glows softly in the light from the instruments in front of her, and it makes her even prettier than she is, with her high cheekbones, sensuous lips and dark eyes. Like most Malaysian women she is not very tall, so she has her seat well forward in order to reach the flight controls comfortably, and she has adjusted the rudder pedals as close as she can. Not that they are used much on a jet airliner, but they are important in crosswind takeoffs and landings, and if an engine fails.

First Officer Nurul Sinna is pilot-flying, PF, so she is in charge of handling the flight controls. Which these days mostly means controlling the many settings and modes on the autopilot because most airlines only allow pilots to hand fly the aircraft for very short periods around takeoff and landing. That may sound like she hasn't got much to do, but the exact opposite is true. Often flying the aircraft through the autopilot is more complicated to get right than hand flying, and requires a lot of planning and concentration. But the autopilot is smoother, smarter and more patient than any human pilot. It gives passengers the ride they want—one they can't feel—and it saves the company fuel.

Sinna only joined Air Batam five years ago, and she is intensely proud to have made first officer on the overseas routes at the young age of 28. Most of her contemporaries are still stuck in regional turboprops on the short hops. Her parents are even prouder, in fact her entire family holds her up so high it's hard to bear sometimes. She is the first to make a success of life away from the village. They all know it has cost her a lot of hard work, and she carefully hides any signs of what else it has cost.

It is just after midnight, and they are flying over a black South China Sea towards Vietnam in the north. Ahead the ocean and sky merge into a big, black hole. Only if Gupta leans forward and looks up can he see the stars; ahead they disappear in the mist like on most night flights this time of year.

Captain Gupta is pilot-not-flying, PNF, which makes him responsible for navigation, communication and the setting and monitoring of aircraft systems. Plus dealing with any anomalies or emergencies that might arise. Those jobs used to keep three pilots busy, but electronics and automation have taken the hard work out of it, and it's now mostly a question of selecting the right screens for display and carefully monitoring the information they present. A bit like a computer game, but at a much slower pace. And with deadlier consequences if he gets it wrong.

The two pilot roles normally alternate between flights except in special circumstances where company Standard Operating Procedures call for the captain to take control. But right now Gupta is relaxed and pleased to see his protégé control the big, complex aircraft with such competence. He even finds it disturbingly erotic.

They have not spoken much in the half hour or so since departure apart from what is needed to do their jobs, but that is not unusual. Departure from a big international airport is a busy time as Standard Instrument Departure procedures are followed to the letter and relief from those restrictions are sought and negotiated in order to save time and therefore money. At four to five hundred US dollars per minute, flying a big airliner brings a whole new meaning to the saying that time is money. Each pilot has a precise role to play in the delicate dance act they are performing in the sky in order to do the best for their passengers, their bosses and ultimately themselves.

But now they have reached their cruising altitude of 35000 feet, or flight level 350, and things are settling down. They are following a highway in the sky called airway M753 with its succession of waypoints.

"Ninety miles to IPRIX," says Gupta, calling out the waypoint where Malaysian airspace ends and Vietnamese takes over. "Twelve minutes."

"OK, anything you want me to do?"

"No, steady as she goes. I'll prompt him if he doesn't call us in the next five minutes." The captain doesn't want to draw attention to their flight, but on the other hand doesn't want to get too close to Vietnamese airspace without clearance. Or, in fact, get into Vietnamese airspace at all. It could be a close call, but he is on top of it.

"Batam 8125, call Ho Chi Minh on one two zero decimal niner, good night." The call from Lumpur Radar comes as expected just as they are coming up to ten miles from IPRIX.

Gupta bites his tongue as he returns his rehearsed response: "All right, good night."

It goes against his instinct and training not to use the standard phrases he learnt in basic training and has used ever since. But this night is not textbook, very far from it. The words he speaks are carefully chosen and rehearsed in order to cause confusion, debate and controversy when this flight is analysed by everybody and their grandma in the coming weeks and months.

4. THE CABIN

Farah hasn't slept all night. First her husband of less than a day made sure she didn't, but even after he exhausted himself and started snoring softly, she couldn't sleep. She was sore; he had been wild and a little brutal. Not at all gentle as he had promised. Maybe she should have let him have his way with her much earlier, heaven knows she wanted to, but even more she wanted it to be the way she had dreamt of from when she was a little girl. Something so precious it couldn't just be given away on a hot whim. So she stood her ground; not until she was married. She knew her friends would laugh at her, so she kept her ideals to herself. It was a bubble, but it was bright and shining and she didn't want it to burst.

Her head is still spinning, not only from the night, but from the day before. It had been like a merry-go-round with a broken brake. Not that she wanted it to stop, just slow down a little; it was all passing in a dizzying blur. The ceremony, the reception, her parents, his parents, the profusion of guests, her own friends and relatives but also friends of the parents that she had never met, the masses of presents, and then in the end the tumult of the shared bed.

Today things have not slowed down much, so she just hangs on as best she can, trying to keep a dignified composure, while Hamizan rushes them through the mad melee of Singapore Changi Airport after checking in what seems to her a mountain of baggage for their six weeks round-the-world honeymoon. She has no idea how they will move all that around with them wherever they go.

He has arranged the tickets through his work and been very secretive about the details. They have worked out the itinerary together, of course, so she knows they are flying to Beijing first, and after four days on to San Francisco. There they'll hire a car and drive across the US in two weeks, spend a week in New York, then fly to London. But after that she can't remember—Paris or Rome? It is more than she ever dreamt of and almost more than she can cope with all at once.

Now they are snaking their way through the jetway, as Hamizan calls the corridor that leads out to the aircraft. They have both flown before, but he many more times than her. She has only been on a couple of holidays with her parents, to nearby Borneo and Java, and once to a seminar in Bangkok with her job.

Up ahead she sees the stewardesses greet passengers and check their boarding passes. Everybody gets warm welcomes and big smiles and are shown in the direction of their seats. Most turn right, but she knows that the few who turn left are businessmen and women who are entering the expensive first or business class at the front of the aircraft where people only travel when others pay for their tickets.

When they get to the door, the air hostess takes their boarding cards which Hamizan has been holding on to secretively. She glances at the cards and beams at the young couple.

"Welcome to Air Batam Mr. bin Emir, Mrs. binti Kamat. Right this way, my colleague will show you to your seats," she says and holds a slim arm out to the left.

Farah is sure there must be a mistake and gives her husband a worried look.

"Hami?"

"It's all right Ari."

He calls her Ari after her other given name, Arissa. Everybody else calls her Farah, but she loves the name he has decided for himself. It's also what her granddad called her beloved grandmother, but Hami doesn't know that. She keeps that hidden away inside with a few other things that make her feel warm and safe.

"We're in business class—all the way round the world." The young man can't contain his pride any longer; he has been looking forward to this more than to his wedding night.

Another flight attendant appears from the forward cabin and greets them as warmly as if they were regular visitors to her rarefied world.

"Welcome on board. Seats 4 J and K," she smiles with a glance at their boarding cards. "This way please sir and madam," and shows them to their two opulent seats on the right side of the cabin.

"Do you want window or aisle?" Hamizan asks Farah.

She looks at the two seats; they are wide enough that both she and Hamizan could fit into one of them, and there is so much leg room they could put another row of seats in the gap. She has never seen anything like it.

"They turn into beds."

"Hami!" she whispers and blushes a little.

The air hostess discreetly lets the young couple chatter on. She has seen it all before and prefers them to the jaded businessmen that she mostly deals with. Or women, they are sometimes the worst.

"No, but they do. It's a night flight, y'know. We'll be sleeping after dinner."

"Dinner?"

"With all the trimmings!"

Then it dawns on her that he is doing all this for her far more than for himself, and she wraps her arms around him.

"Oh, Hami! It's so wonderful. How have you done it?"

"I'll tell you later. Window or aisle, madam?"

*

The meeting Ariel Beckman has just come from didn't go well. It was only meant to be a courtesy call really, stopping off on his way to Beijing to see an old client in Singapore and confirm business as usual and grease the wheels a little. But it turned sour. Ariel is what they used to call a travelling salesman, but he considers himself way above sales and would never accept that description. Consultant, if you please. In waste management of all things, so some people call him Binman behind his back. Which he would never dignify with a reply.

Waste is big business, always has been, but Ariel Beckman is not a nightman or a scrap metal merchant. Nothing as sordid as that. He is into the really big business, and today that is not waste storage, collection or transport. Or even waste treatment, recycling or reuse. The real money is in the planning, the education and the training that is needed to do all the other things. That's what the company Ariel Beckman works for, Waste Management Training—Wamat for short—does.

Ecology and sustainability are the buzzwords, and anyone with a cleaner or cheaper way, or preferably both, to treat the mountains of unwanted stuff the modern world produces effectively has his own private, and perfectly legal, money printing press. Perth-based Wamat was an early player in this lucrative field and quickly expanded from its Australian home market to Indonesia, the Philippines and Malaysia. And now they have their sights set on the biggest market in the world, China.

It's on the way there that Ariel stopped off to see an old client. An old friend even. Trouble is, the friend is a lot older than Ariel and has a son who is a lot younger. That's where it all went wrong. The son has new ideas about how to train his workers himself, and contacts to American companies with cheaper methods than Wamat's. Ariel knows it's mostly a way to bicker about costs, but he can do without young whippersnappers reminding him that the scene is getting crowded.

He doesn't need that on his way to China. China is supposed to be the land of milk and honey these days. He doesn't want to be reminded that there are younger, leaner companies out there and that they are probably already talking to the same customers he is going to see.

As if that isn't enough, now Air Batam no longer offer first class on most of their routes. Ariel is a long time fan of Air Batam, but not of their modernisation. OK, to be fair their new business class is almost as good as first class used to be. In fact the seats are better, they turn into proper, flat beds long enough for a grown man. And the service is the same. Professional, perfect, the way only Orientals can do it. He never knows what they think behind their masks, but as long as they look pretty and suck up to him, he doesn't mind. The food is slightly less opulent than it used to be; no more Beluga caviar ad libitum. Never mind, you can't get the real stuff any more, only farmed and it's not the same.

No, the real sting is the loss of prestige. First class is for people who have arrived, like owning a Rolls Royce, and turning left at the end of the jetway used to be the preserve of first class passengers. Business was to the right, along with the peasants in the back. But that was on the good old 747s, a world away. Oh, the old workhorses are still there, but airlines have taken the upper deck bar out, with its big U-shaped sofa, and stuffed it full of seats. And the biggest beast in the sky is now an air bus, for crying out loud.

Ariel looks at the queue up ahead and allows himself to enjoy the little scene with a young couple who are getting upgraded to business for some reason. The woman clearly expected to go into tourist class. Must know someone who knows someone; always the way it works. He doesn't mind upgraders as long as they haven't got a screaming kid, and these two don't look like they have got that far yet, though not for the want of trying. Then it strikes him. Honeymooners. No doubt. The recognition shoots through him like a white-hot bolt and he nearly stumbles when the line moves a step ahead. It was such a long time ago.

"Welcome on Air Batam again Mr. Beckman. Right this way sir, my colleague will show you to your seat," the air hostess greets him and holds her slim hand out to the hallowed left.

Again? How does that pretty girl know he has been there before? The boarding card has a small dot that nobody notices to show cabin crew that this is a frequent flyer. It works, and even old, jaded Ariel Beckman feels a sudden pang.

"Welcome on board, sir. Seat 3K," her colleague smiles. With a glance on his boarding card, she shows him to his seat. "This way please Mr. Beckman."

The honeymoon couple are in the seats behind his, and he arrives just as the young woman embraces her new husband. Gotta be her brand new husband, no doubt about it. Ariel steels himself a little. Keep it together old man. But he feels himself melting away on the inside because he knows he is witnessing something he once had himself but was stupid enough to lose. He wants to scream at the young man to hold her close, to never let her go. To not be an idiot like he was, like everyone else is. Then he dumps his big body into seat 3K and pretends to have an attack of the coughs while he desperately fumbles for a handkerchief to wipe away those damn tears. Where's that bloody champagne they always ply you with?

*

Ling Yang is trying to hold it all together, but around her all is chaos and she is losing her grip. The unfamiliar sounds of the big departure hall, the pushing and shoving of thousands of people who are either late or afraid of being late. Even the all-pervading smells of the Orient that she has half forgotten.

Ling has left three-year old Jasmine with her own mother while she and her husband check the bags in. "Stay right here so we can find you again," she had said, but now they are nowhere to be seen.

33

"Jiei, can you see them anywhere?"

"No, why didn't you tell your mother to stay put?"

"I did. I told her to stay right here. Where can she be? How long do we have?"

"Half an hour, but it's a long walk to the gate. Why hasn't she got a cellphone?"

"You know she can't use one. She still hates the buttons on her phone at home; she wants her dial back." Ling briefly sees the comic side, that's the way she deals with the world, but quickly returns to the reality of a flight that could soon leave without them.

"Bathrooms. Gotta be the bathrooms. You check out the Ladies," William says.

"Where? They are all over the place."

"Follow the signs to the nearest, that's what she'll have done."

"You stay here!"

"Sure. Got your phone?"

"Yes."

"Switched on?"

"Yes."

"Not on silent?"

"Stop it Jie, it's not funny."

"I thought it was." He looks hurt, just to cheer her up.

"There they are!"

"Sorry. She had to go." The old woman is breathless and dishevelled, which is very much against her nature. She is proud of her neat and tidy appearance and spends a long time on it. Now it's all gone, just because the child needed a wee. Why couldn't they have done that at home?

It is only the third time she sees her grandchild. Her daughter and son-in-law live in Los Angeles and she doesn't like travelling, particularly not flying. William Jie Yang, her son-in-law, is a Chinese American as they call it over there (she supposes that makes her a Chinese Malaysian), and more American than the Americans. Doesn't even read Chinese and speaks it very little, and very badly. Ling, her daughter, met him while studying at the big university they call UCLA which she thinks sounds like some primitive war cry, and married him in spite of her mother's misgivings. Not about the man, but about the country.

"Not your people," she had told her daughter. "Not your culture. In fact, no culture at all."

"Mom, it doesn't matter. We love each other. Besides, it's not all that bad. LA has both a ballet and an opera. The ballet even has a Danish director, how cool is that?"

LA. Cool. There it was again, the slang, the vulgar pandering to the lowest common denominator. She didn't exactly hate America, only the way people there behaved.

"I know you love him. Does he love you the same way?"

"Yes he does." Ling was a little defensive.

"How do you know?"

"Mom!"

"I want to know. It's important, please tell me." She nearly followed up with a "I'm your mother," but bit her tongue just in time.

"By the way he looks at me. And the way he touches me." The young woman was telling her mother things she barely knew she knew herself, but now she did.

"Then that's all that matters, I know that," the old woman said quietly and took her daughter's hand.

She did. She had been in a loveless arranged marriage for forty years, so she knew. She had tried to make it work, and succeeded after a fashion. Tried to find love and make it grow, but it always came back to the cruel fact that there was no real love there to begin with. There was tenderness sometimes, and shared interests in the children that soon came. But not the inner glow she thought should be there. Not that she had ever felt that for anyone else either, and sometimes she wondered if she lacked the ability. Even with her children there was from time to time a glass wall she couldn't see but also couldn't reach through. She worked hard for nobody to find out, and that often just made it worse.

In the end her daughter married her American, her Chinese American. And a few years later came little Jasmine, called Yan after her great grandmother. She knew they had done that to win her over, and it worked. She only wished Ling had kept her maiden name, Wong, but she had chosen the Western way of taking her husband's name, Yang.

"Come on, we've got to hurry. We gotta be at the gate in twenty."

Not "twenty minutes." She grits her teeth. Or is it just his bad Chinese?

She sets in motion with as much decorum as she can muster at this point. At least age has one benefit: people may want to hurry you along, but their exasperation is usually tempered by a deference to age that has not quite left the young. Maybe not real respect any more, but a vague feeling that one day it's going to be their turn. She uses that to good effect.

They arrive at the jetway just as the ground hostess is about to call operations and ask for a passenger announcement, and are the last to board the big jet. Yan takes it all in her stride. She rides in her baby buggy and happily sucks her thumb. She knows she is getting too old for both, but enjoys getting away with it, as she does when her mom and dad get all worked up.

"Welcome to Air Batam, sir, madams, young lady." The smile is still there even if it is a little paler and the eyes a little more vacant. It's past gate time, and they need to get a move on.

"Row thirty, please. It's just along this aisle and to the left past the galley." She wonders briefly if the American has paid extra for the first row behind the galley to squeeze a bit more legroom out of tourist class or they have been given those seats because of the child. Whatever. They look like a nice enough family, if only granny would be a little quicker on the move.

The little family enter by the middle door and have only a short walk to row 30, which is the first row of the second section of tightly packed tourist class seats, and they set about finding space for their cabin bags and overcoats. There is no room in the overhead lockers, so he looks round for help from a cabin attendant.

"Looks like we've got all five seats to ourselves," his wife says.

William eyes a chance to angle his lanky six foot four frame across two seats. Flying is hard for tall people, especially flying in the back of the sardine cans which is all anyone can afford these days. He wishes there were a middle ground, one without the opulence and gluttony but with enough room for real people. He doesn't know how he got to be so tall. His mother used to say it was the air in America. Or the Bomb. Both his parents, second generation Chinese emigrants, were as small as their parents before them.

"Then Yan can get some proper sleep. The armrest folds up so she can lie across two seats. Let's ask the stewardess." Ling looks around the cabin.

William knows that very well, that's what he had had in mind for himself, but he is wise enough not to argue. Besides, Ling is right. Yan is up way past her bedtime and the sooner she settles down the better for all concerned.

"'Scuse me miss, will we have this row to ourselves? It's just that our daughter could use two seats for a bed if nobody else is in it." He feels he has to justify himself, but of course the stewardess isn't a mind reader and doesn't know he had been thinking of those two seats for himself.

"Looks like it, sir. It's best if she could use the seatbelt while she sleeps, though. Let me know if you need a child belt."

"Thanks. Any chance you can find somewhere for our bags? There's no room up there."

"I'll take it, sir. I can fit it in the coat closet."

"Thanks very much."

The whole cabin is relieved when they settle down in their seats. They place Yan between her mother and grandmother. William wants to be close to his daughter too, but realises it's important that the child and the old lady get as much time together as possible. This trip is all about family, his wife's family mostly, but he will be meeting up with distant relatives too. It's a strange new world with new rules and new opportunities emerging almost every day, and he is determined that his daughter will grow up a citizen of the world and not of just one nation.

Being an American used to be the best thing he could think of, the most wonderful birthright in the world if you were lucky enough to have it. But he is having doubts now. There is something about it that smacks of smug self-satisfaction, of to hell with the rest, which he finds quite unpleasant at times.

Yan will be an American for sure, but an American with wide horizons. That's the best he can do for her.

5. THE WAR GAME

We rolled out TheWar a year later, at the end of 2007. We'd put a lot of work into it, Omar and I, and it was getting to be everything we had planned for. There were still things we needed to add, but the game had become massively popular in a very short time. Now, a year later, it had over twenty million users and counting.

That sort of growth could only happen on the internet, where things spread like wildfire by word-of-mouth if they were any good. It was the law of binary numbers—one user told two friends who each told two friends and so on. Fifteen steps later over thirty thousand people knew about it, after twenty steps, over a million, and after 25, over 30 million. OK, they didn't all pass it on, but many people told a lot more than two friends, so it actually worked out pretty much like that. Those people were already into gaming, or their friends wouldn't have told them about it, so the uptake was high.

It helped a lot that it was free, of course. The expectation on the internet was still that everything was free, and very few had yet worked out how to run a real business in cyberspace. Blowing dotcom bubbles was as far as it went, and most of those had burst. The internet was mostly one big playground, and TheWar fed right into that concept. There were also some very dark sides to the net, everything from kiddie porn to Ponzi schemes, but they operated in the deep shadows of a system that was not well understood and kept transforming itself all the time. In that framework, we would be free to evolve TheWar in any direction we wanted.

By late 2008 we had got to the stage where the game was running smoothly and we had time to think about what else to do with it. We still hadn't made any money from it, and we were starting to have second thoughts about that. It seemed a little banal to go down that route, I mean just doing what everybody else does, milking others for their money. TheWar was beginning to have a community feel to it, and there had to be something smarter to do with it than just make it commercial.

"Hi Nige, I'm home."

His tone hit me like hammer. The fact that he was home in the middle of a Monday afternoon hit me like a hammer. He had to be sick. That voice! Oh God, something was wrong. Had he been to see his doctor? Did he have AIDS? Cancer?

Omar was standing just inside the front door as if he had never been here before and didn't know where to go next. His beautiful golden complexion was gone. I had never seen him like that. He looked like dirty dishwater. I was unable to move, just like he was. I knew my life, our lives, were changing. Right then and there.

"They fired me," he stammered. "They fired everybody."

The relief nearly made me lose my balance, and I had to lean against the corridor wall.

"Ome, for fuck's sake. I thought you were dying."

We looked at each other across the few feet of corridor. Then I grabbed him and held on tight.

"They called a staff meeting at two, everybody had to be there, all meetings cancelled, phones on voicemail, nobody knew what it was, we'd heard the Lehman bank in New York had collapsed and administrators had turned up at their London office, but we didn't know that had anything to do with us, then they told us they were closing down, their bank had called in all their loans and closed all their accounts because Lehman had called in theirs, they were bust, nobody had a job anymore, not even salaries for this month, some of the guys had pensions too, all gone, all fucking gone man, just like that."

We were sitting in the sofa, and it was all gushing out of him. He had never lost a job before, so losing one in this way was hitting him hard. But he was getting some of his colour back. I could hear what he was saying, but I wanted to shout "So what? It's a job! You'll get another. You're a genius. They all know that." But I knew it wasn't necessarily as simple as that. Not any more. It was what he said next that hit me hard.

"And I can only stay here as long as I have work!"

It had all seemed so easy. Everybody and his uncle were emigrating to England, so what's the problem? An American, for crying out loud. Special relationship and all that. But Omar was here on a work permit and could only stay as long as he had a job that qualified.

"You'll find work. There's going to be a line a mile long."

"Yeah, and I'll be standing in it. Don't you know what's happening out there?"

I knew. It had been a while since I had had any work to speak of, and that had been short patch-up jobs. Companies were careful with their cash after the cheap credit had started to dry up the year before. Northern Rock had been bailed out by the British government, and big banks all over the world were announcing eye-watering losses. We all thought it would pass, but it only seemed to get worse. Lehman began to look like the start of an avalanche.

"Ome, we'll think of something. You and me, we'll never be out of work, not for long. And we can live for a while on what we have." Because of my irregular work, I had built up a cushion, and it had grown reasonably in the good years, and our outgoings weren't all that high.

"We could've lost all that," he said.

"I know, but we didn't. It's safe now. Spread out so it's all guaranteed. We'll make it work." Our hearts and minds had never been in bricks and mortar; we had built our lives round other values, and that made us less vulnerable now incomes were coming under pressure.

"But I have to have a job. My visa says so."

"If you can't find one, I'll set up a company and hire you."

"Would that work?"

"Not sure, but yes, I think it would. Why not? We'll get some advice. Man, I'm so relieved. I thought you were dying or something." I couldn't get the shock out of my system, but I could see it hurt him that I thought losing his job was no big deal.

"Ome, listen. I'm sorry you lost your job, and I'm sorry the way it happened. I know it's a blow, but we'll work something out. I promise. We'll work something out together."

"Yeah, you're right. It's just not something I'm used to. C'mon, I need some fresh air. I'll buy you a pint." When he came to London, Omar had no idea what a "pint" was, other than an eighth of a gallon, but he quickly found out it's something you get in your pub when you're thirsty. And you had to have a pub.

When we came back, I switched on the TV while I started cooking dinner, and we watched scenes unfolding in both London and New York with Lehman Brothers employees carrying cardboard boxes out of glass skyscrapers. The contrast between those mighty towers and the sad little possessions people were allowed to take with them was so stark it was surreal.

"It's all coming down," I said. "It's all coming effing tumbling down."

We looked on in silence for a while. We didn't know what to say. I was beginning to get scared, but didn't say anything. There's nothing like fear to spread and grow, so you've got to keep a lid on it. But I was beginning to think, That's it. The end. Not of the world, but of the world as we know it. This is what the terrorists couldn't do, but now the bastards have done it to themselves.

Later on there were reports of bankers jumping out of offices in tall buildings.

"It's 9/11 all over again, without the dust," Omar said and instinctively made a move as if to brush off the dust that he'd been caught in that day.

"I think this could be a lot worse," I said. "I think this could actually do what they failed to do back then. Look at those guys. There's no fight in them. On 9/11 everybody stood up and fought back, but now they're just packing up and going home." I regretted it the moment I said it.

"I know the feeling." His tone was sharp.

"Sorry Ome. Sorry, I know. But don't you see?" It came to me in a flash, one of those moments when you feel you suddenly know something nobody else does. I didn't see all the details, but the idea was there. That was what I was good at, getting ideas.

"See what?"

"That this is the Achilles' heel of the whole Western world. The banking system. Nobody thought it was that fragile."

"I know what fragile feels like," he said.

I couldn't say anything right that evening, so I shut up and got on with the cooking.

*

TheWar came to our rescue. The game still didn't make any money, but it provided the background to set up a company that looked real. An internet game with millions of players—not so long ago that would have been worth a lot of dotcom money, but now at least I hoped it could convincingly give Omar the job he needed to stay in the UK, even if there was no real income except what I paid in and he took straight out again, just to keep everybody happy. We'd have to work on that somehow.

There was plenty of money in the game by the way, it just wasn't real money. We'd come up with the idea of digital money that only existed in the game, and it turned out to be a surprisingly effective way both to attract players and to manipulate them. We could see the uptake curve rise steeply when we rolled out dMon, as we called our digital currency.

That was my idea too, of course.

"dMon, demon, mammon, don't you get it?" My voice was breaking with exasperation. Sometimes Omar was deliberately slow on the uptake just to wind me up, but this time he was downright stubborn. He wanted it to be something that sounded like a real currency.

"Sounds like toy money."

"It IS toy money."

"That's precisely why it shouldn't SOUND like toy money."

I left it there for a while and simply started to put dMons into my code. Not the code the players were using, but what I sent to our alpha and beta testers.

The testers loved it, and by the time we were getting feedback, it was almost Omar's idea. Only almost, he didn't dare go quite that far this time, but he pretended to have backed it all the way. That was fine with me.

*

It was pitch dark, so it must have been the noise that woke me. The door bell was ringing like mad, there was hammering on the door and I could hear people shouting outside, but not their words. I reached out for Omar, but he was out cold, deaf and blind to the world behind his eyeshades and earplugs.

The ringing and the knocking stopped and I thought for a moment it had been a bad dream. Then there was a colossal crash that sounded like a train hit the house. The bed shook and wild roars came from the corridor. My brain shut down, but my arms and hands were desperately grappling for something to cover myself with. We slept naked, and that made me feel even more helpless.

Then the bedroom door was violently kicked open and I was blinded by two intensely bright lights. I couldn't see the men who held them, just the lights. But now I could hear them.

"ARMED POLICE STAY STILL. DO NOT MOVE."

I didn't move a muscle, I was stiff with terror. Omar was sleeping through it all.

"OMAR FARID. ARE YOU OMAR FARID?"

"No, I'm Nigel. Taylor. Omar's there." I tried to move an arm to point behind me, but I only managed an awkward jerk.

"STAY STILL I SAID. IS HE BEHIND YOU IN THE BED?"

"Yes." I wanted to say that he was sleeping with shades and earplugs, but I was seizing up with the terror of it all and couldn't get the words out. I could hear the crashing and banging continue outside the bedroom door; somebody was tearing our little home apart.

One black, burly figure kept a light in my face, still blinding me, and the other moved round the bed.

"OMAR FARID, ARE YOU OMAR FARID?" He was still shouting at the top of his voice, as if to deliberately keep the terror at full pitch.

I had no idea how Omar would react to being suddenly jerked awake in the middle of this insane pandemonium. He was not a violent man by any stretch of the imagination, but we all have deep-seated animal reactions. His was, when he was finally woken by the screaming and the bright lights in his face, to throw himself at his assailant with arms going like a windmill. The flashlight crashed to the floor and rolled under the bed. I had turned sideways to look away from the light which was hurting

48

my eyes but could only see a dark mass at the foot of the bed. Then I heard Omar screaming.

"WADDAYA DOING? LET GO MY FUCKING ARM. WHAT THE FUCK IS THIS? WHO ARE YOU? AARRRGH, YOU'RE BREAKING MY ARM. NIGEL, NIGEL, HE'S BREAKING MY AAAARM."

I heard it snap with a sound like when you step on a dry branch on the forest floor. I also heard a deeper, crunching sound like walking across pebbles on a beach.

"STAY STILL BOTH OF YOU. ARMED POLICE. OMAR FARID YOU ARE UNDER ARREST. YOU DO NOT HAVE TO SAY ANYTHING BUT IT MAY HARM YOUR DEFENCE IF YOU DO NOT MENTION WHEN QUESTIONED SOMETHING WHICH YOU LATER RELY ON IN COURT. ANYTHING YOU DO SAY MAY BE GIVEN IN EVIDENCE."

Omar didn't say anything. I only heard him whimpering. The light was still blinding me. But my brain was starting to work again.

"WHAT *IS* THIS?" I screamed. "ARE YOU FUCKING OUT OF YOUR MINDS?"

"I'll arrest you too if you don't stop swearing at a police officer."

"I have no f…" I just managed to check myself "idea who you are. I have no idea what's going on. WHAT *IS* THIS?" I was starting to cry hysterically and tried desperately to cover my nakedness.

"We are Metropolitan Police Counter Terrorism Command. Omar Farid is under arrest for offences under the Terrorism Act. Put some clothes on, you fucking fag."

I was suddenly violently sick all over myself and the bed and the fucking filth.

*

In the beginning we thought it had something to do with Omar's work permit or his visa, and we even thought it was our own fault for not dealing with that properly. But Immigration had nothing to do with it. It turned out they had never even registered the fact that the company he was supposed to work for had gone bust, or who he was working for now, or even if he worked for anyone. In fact, they seemed to know or care little about him.

It would have been better if they had, because it just might have stopped what happened next. Which was an almighty British cock-up. This was 2009, four years after they shot dead a Brazilian tourist in the subway over mistaken identity, and they didn't seem to have learned a thing.

They had taken my mild-mannered, totally harmless Omar for another Omar Farid, from Yemen, who was supposed to be an extremely dangerous individual. We never found out how they managed to do that; they stonewalled streams of requests from our lawyers and the media to release details about it. Official secrets, they said. The media briefly clamoured for the Police Commissioner to step down, but then the next government scandal broke and the press went off in pursuit of that.

As long as the press were on their back, the police didn't seem to try too hard to wriggle out of compensating Omar for his broken back.

That was the crunching sound I heard the morning the terror police came and put a knee into the small of Omar's back to hold him down, crushing his first lumbar vertebra and his spinal cord. They said it was an accident and that he was partly to blame for resisting arrest. They said they would never do that on purpose, but it happened in the heat of the struggle to control him.

And as soon as it became yesterday's news, their lawyers hired a consultant orthopaedic surgeon to testify that Omar had had osteoporosis all along and that his broken back had absolutely nothing to do with a 250-pound policeman trampling on it. It was all his own fault for being such a pathetic, unhealthy, vitamin D deficient nerd. Not to mention gay, so they didn't, but they did test for AIDS in case they could have used that against him too.

Once one consultant pronounced on the case, nobody else wanted to touch it. We searched high and low, but they were all too busy, or did not have the exact right expertise, or were just going on holiday or had just returned from one and had other commitments, or simply didn't reply.

So in the end, Omar's compensation claim was refused and we were left to fend for ourselves. On top of that, just to really rub salt in the wound, they fought our complaints about homophobic abuse tooth and nail. We could not prove how we had been treated when they found two naked blokes in bed together. It was only the word of a skinny, pasty and spotty fag against the boys in blue. We never stood a chance.

The arm healed, but the back didn't. Omar was left paralysed from the waist down. He was having operations and therapy, and nobody said it would be for life, but that didn't really matter at the time.

What mattered was that they had crushed more than his back. They had crushed the man. A man who had never done anyone any harm, and never would have. They had turned genius and passion into anger and bitterness. And fear. He had fierce escape reflexes at the slightest unexpected noise and went into a panic every time because he couldn't move. He was having therapy for that too, and he had to take strong pills to sleep at night.

There wasn't a therapy or treatment or medicine he didn't have, but none of it brought him back. My bright and sunny and quick-witted Omar could no longer see any good in anything or anyone.

With the one possible exception of me.

*

"Have you looked at the user figures lately?" I asked him one morning.

"No." He didn't sound interested.

"Ome, if you started working on it again, it would give you something to do." He had hardly touched his computer since that terrible night. It had been more than a year, it was now late 2010, and I was running out of things to try to cheer him up with, or at least keep him from brooding. He was brooding far too much, but I was still working from home most of the time, so I tried to stop it when I saw it coming.

"But I've been thinking," he said. "Remember what you said about 9/11 not working?"

"Errr, not sure when I said that, but yeah, I don't believe it did."

"Nige, will you promise me that what I say now stays between us? I'd ask you to swear if you believed in anything."

"That serious?"

"That serious."

"Of course I will Ome. I promise. Cross my heart and hope to die." I tried to make light of it. He was scaring me a little.

"I've actually been thinking a lot about the game, and I think I have an idea how we could use it. If we wanted to." He lowered his head and raised his eyes to look across at me as he did when he was unsure of himself.

"In what way?"

"Well, what you were saying about 9/11."

I could hear he was feeling me out for some reason.

"Out with it, Ome. I've promise it won't go any further. Not even if you've turned terrorist for real."

"That's just it. Maybe I have."

My jaw dropped. "What, blow things up?"

He grimaced. "Of course not. That doesn't work. People have done that for centuries, and we know it doesn't work. At least those of us with some brain can see that it doesn't. Flying airliners into buildings doesn't work either. But you know what could change the world?"

"Tell me."

"You and I could. I think. At least we could try."

"You're being evasive. And pompous, but tell me."

"With our computer skills."

"Hacking? Cyber war? Thousands are doing that, tens of thousands. Governments are spending millions planning to do it, or already doing it. Nobody has done any real or lasting damage yet. OK, maybe some damage that costs somebody some money, or a lot of money, but change the world? No."

"I know. I'm not talking about hacking. Or about cyber war. Not in the conventional sense."

"What then?"

"TheWar."

"Sorry, you lost me. It's a game. It's a very popular game, but it's a game."

"Exactly, and that's why we could get away with it. Everybody will just think it's a game. They won't take it seriously. Nobody keeps an eye on the online games; they think it all happens on the social networks."

"You lost me again. It IS just a game."

"Yes, but what if we turned it into more than just a game?"

"Ome, you'll have to spell it out. I'll tell you if I like it or not, and if I'll do it or not, and I won't tell anyone else about it, but you got to stop messing me about."

"Sure, but so far it's just an idea, OK? Some of it is your own, you just don't know it. You said a couple of years ago that the Achilles' heel of Western capitalism is the banking system when they nearly crashed it themselves."

"Yes. But they're getting over that, too."

"Hang on. You also said, a long time ago, that the problem with 9/11 was no follow-through."

"Did I? Jeez, you remember everything I say? But yes, that's what I still think. So you want the banks to keep shooting themselves in the foot?"

"Well, they'll keep doing that without our help. But I'm thinking of giving them a bit more of a push. And then another, and then another, as many as they need. The follow-through."

"How?"

"By making things happen that put banks under pressure. And making it keep happening until they collapse. All of them. When the big ones go, they all go. It'll be a chain reaction."

"Sorry to sound like a broken record, but how?"

"By training and motivating people in key positions to do certain things."

"What, for instance."

"OK, look what happened when that volcano blew up in Iceland back in April. Eyafjallawhatever. I've been reading up on it. It was just six days, but nearly a hundred thousand flights were cancelled—a HUNDRED THOUSAND—the airlines lost billions, oil companies lost hundreds of millions, shares dropped. And that was only six days worth of flying, in one corner of the world. Aviation is key to almost everything else, and it's bloody fragile. Just a little dust. Or even the risk of a little dust."

"Yes, OK, but we can't control volcanoes."

"No, not volcanoes, but other things could hit them just as hard."

"I suppose."

"Anyway, I haven't worked out the all details, we need to do that together. If you want to."

"No blowing things up?"

"Promise, no blowing up. Scout's honour." He held up three fingers.

"You've never been a scout. Sorry, I'm still not clear on the how."

"Here's what I'm thinking. We could use TheWar to find people who are well placed and impressionable. We already have some psychological profiling of players. We could expand that. Concentrate on players we can, errm, influence. Program. Call it brainwash if you will. Those who are already angry or disaffected or marginalised. Those with buttons we can push. We could then start pushing those buttons and give them the training they need to make things happen that we want to happen."

"You said no bombs."

"I'm not talking about bombs. How many times do I have to say it? Bombs don't work. History shows they don't. I'm talking about switching things off and scaring people and stopping things working. Putting spokes in wheels that make key industries go round. Enough to make the financial system crumble from within. I think the key is aviation, and the key to that is to make people so afraid of flying that they stop. That would put enormous pressure on banks, especially while they are as wobbly as they are now.

"Yes, but…"

"No, let me finish. It could start an avalanche with other industries following, oil, food, shipping. That's the biggie. Won't stop the ships as such, they are pretty hard to get to. Look at how little effect a whole army of Somalian pirates have, except on the poor bastards they hold to ransom. But it'll all break down pretty quickly if they can't fly their crews around."

"I think shipping's a lot more volatile than that," I interrupted him.

"How's that?"

"One of the financial packages I made for United Grocers tracks a number of industry indices to predict futures. One of those indices is called the Baltic Dry Index, BDI. It tracks the cost of shipping dry raw materials around the world in bulk, things like grain, metal ore, chemicals, coal. For many years it was drifting up and down about plus/minus 50 percent according to market conditions. If more goods needed shipping than could be handled by the available fleet, shipping costs went up, then people built more ships and costs went down again. It was roughly an 18 to 24 month cycle, in tune with the time it takes to build ships."

"Doesn't sound all that volatile."

"Not until around 2002, but then it all went completely nuts. Prices trebled in a couple of years, then crashed back again in 2006, then rose *ten* times by 2007-8, then crashed by about 95% with the banking crisis at the end of 2008. All because market forces got out of whack. If markets get really spooked for one reason or another, shipping is one of the first to feel the effects, and they are huge. *That* would put a lot of extra pressure on the banks."

"That's exactly what we're looking for," Omar replied, his eyes shining. "Knock-on effects. Stopping people flying all over the place will be just the start, and everything that follows from that really could do what centuries of stupid, inept terror hasn't done, and with a lot less casualties. We could change the world and cut Western capitalism down to size."

I hadn't seen him that fired up since they broke his back. "When I said no bombs, I meant no-one gets hurt."

"Don't talk to me about getting hurt."

"Ome, we can't do something like this for revenge. And it won't make you walk."

"It's not revenge, or at least not just revenge. I've always wanted to make a difference, and so have you. I don't think it's revenge to want to prevent the motherfuckers who did this to me doing it to someone else. Revenge would be to find a way to break THEIR fucking backs, but that's not what I'm doing. Maybe you can't make an omelette without breaking eggs, but that's not the purpose here. In fact the purpose is the exact opposite. To hurt as few as possible and help as many as possible. The old terror got that wrong, that's why it didn't work, don't you see? If intelligent people like us don't do something smart like this, then some moron will do something stupid that'll hurt a lot more people."

I did see, but I was quiet for a long time. I didn't know what to say. He was clearly pressing my buttons, the way he was planning to use the game to press a lot of other people's buttons. I did share those views, I did think it was wrong for one culture to dominate all others, to rob of them of their natural resources, to use oceans as rubbish dumps, to cut down swathes of forests, to kill off one species of animal after another.

I did feel all that. Very strongly. But would I do anything about it now that I had a chance, or was I just a big mouth?

6. THE FLIGHT DECK

Captain Agung Gupta does not contact Ho Chi Minh control as instructed, even if it is next on his flight plan, because he has no intention of entering Vietnamese airspace at all. If he doesn't, nothing is likely to happen, at least not for a long while. The Vietnamese controller will expect a call but if it does not come, it could be for any number of reasons. Delayed departure, diversion or return because of technical problems are just a few of them. When that happens, the information should be passed on to controllers along the route but that's sometimes delayed or missed, especially between controllers of different countries, or at night when there are fewer controllers on duty and each covers larger areas. That's because there's less traffic at night, but the result can be that controllers work harder than during the day. Anyway, each controller is only responsible for the flights that arrive in his or her airspace, not the ones that don't arrive, whatever the reason may be.

Gupta looks down at the console that separates the two pilots with its sea of knobs, buttons and displays, each with a very specific and important function. He reaches across to the transponder and switches it to Standby.

He then moves to the multifunction display and brings up the Systems page with a few pushes of the buttons. There he selects Standby on the ACARS system that sends data back to the airline once every hour with details on the progress of the flight, the fuel state, the health of the engines and other information used by the company for administration and maintenance. ACARS is a kind of automated aviation email system used for these mundane and non-urgent communications but not for navigation or air traffic control, so it won't be missed by anyone at this time of night. But it is important that it stops sending back data that could give away any clues later on.

Disabling the transponder makes the aircraft harder to track on radar, which is the first part of the plan, but the captain overlooks the separate page controlling the satellite communications subsystem that ACARS uses in remote regions. Maybe he didn't listen properly to his ground instructor that hot and sticky afternoon when the bored class was told about how and when and why ACARS uses satellites when it can't get a VHF radio connection, which is preferred because it's cheaper, but only works over land. There's only so much a chap can be expected to take on board. Besides, he has no reason to think of it. This aircraft doesn't have satellite phones or internet in the cabin, so the system is not a part of the crew's normal awareness.

The captain would also have liked to disable the aircraft's two 'black boxes:' the flight data and cockpit voice recorders, but he can't. Pilots can no longer control them because of the risk of intentional deactivation of this vital safety equipment, either under threat from terrorists or by pilots who feel they are being snooped on by the airline. Even the circuit breaker fuses that protect the boxes are now out of reach of pilots.

Then he straightens up in his seat and turns to look at his co-pilot. He needs to be sure of his situation before he starts down a path of no return, and most importantly of First Officer Sinna's courage and commitment.

Her soft profile is calm and professional, but memories of the excitement they have shared on layovers tingle under his skin. That's one reason why they are where they are now, together on this mission. They know and trust each other. And they are trusted by others because of their secret.

*

Agung would never have started spending so much time with his much younger co-pilot if they hadn't both become addicted to computer gaming. Agung started gaming a few years back when his wife gave him a laptop to while away the time on stopovers. If you don't drink and don't jump into bed with anything in a skirt that happens to be within reach, as Agung didn't, the repeated, long layovers on international destinations can become incredibly difficult to cope with. Agung used to get out and about as much as he could on stopovers and enjoy the sights, but after a while that got repetitive, and quite honestly also tiring as he got older.

He began to look for something he could spend a little time on to relax him enough to get the rest he needed at the odd hours that international aviation forces on its crews. He was one of those pilots who couldn't get enough of flying, and at home he had a full flight simulator setup using his powerful desktop computer with three big screens giving him almost the same wraparound view he knew from his real flight deck. He was thrilled when he thought he could start bringing that with him, but it didn't work all that well on the small computer without the extra screens and flight controls he had hooked up to his home computer. As he couldn't take those with him everywhere, he started seeking more rewarding things to do with his laptop. All the crew hotels had free internet connection, and that's where he went to look for something to while away the time.

One of the things he came across was a game called TheWar, a role-play game where you could take on any role you wanted. If the role you wanted didn't exist, they would create it for you. Very lifelike, you would have to start at the bottom and work your way up, and your training would cost you money, in the game's own digital currency called dMon, which you would have to borrow and pay back when you started "working" in your chosen role.

Agung chose to be a pilot, of course, and had great fun reliving his entire pilot training, from basic flying school through commercial, instrument and airline pilot licences, and even some aerobatics. It was all veryds realistic and he found himself more pleased when after six months he was awarded the title Warrior Pilot than he was with his real world qualification as an Airline Transport Pilot and his job as an airline captain. It was so silly he didn't tell anyone about it, but he started spending more and more time on the game.

TheWar appealed to the little boy within him who kept wanting to be praised, and as a Warrior Pilot he was one of the most important players in TheWar game. Not only did his flying have a huge impact on the battles, but he was also called on by the Council of Warlords for tactical and strategic advice. One of the Warlords was a pilot himself and used Agung as his personal advisor. Not as Captain Agung Gupta, of course, but as Warrior Pilot Arthur Harris. Agung had chosen that name because of his admiration for Britain's Second World War bomber commander whom he felt had been unjustly treated both by his contemporaries and by history. Agung would have bombed even more than the real Harris, and now he had the chance to show those fascists what real war was like.

It was several months after he had started flying regularly with his new first officer Nurul Sinna that one night over dinner they happened to start talking about computers and games. He couldn't believe that she was also playing TheWar and that she was also a Warrior Pilot, third grade, and he had now advanced to first grade, but they both found this exciting. Quite naturally, and totally innocently, they took to playing next to each other in his or her hotel room. The game was designed to let a number of players, who were in the same room, work together more closely and do things they couldn't otherwise do.

Agung resisted for a long time. He had deliberately made himself almost immune to Nurul's alluring presence in the cockpit on one long flight after another, but when he found himself not only working with her but spending more and more of his free time with her too, it became more than he could handle.

When they finally fell into bed with each other, they erupted like volcanoes. He made love like he hadn't done since he was half his age. His stomach was in a knot and his head was spinning and his skin sizzling with it for days afterwards, and he had to feign a man-flu when he got home. Not that it made him love or desire his wife any less, very much the opposite, but he knew he wouldn't be able to hold back, and she would feel the change in him. He was a man on fire.

It was all he could do to keep working, and when he wasn't with Nurul, he escaped into TheWar as an outlet for all this new and frightening energy. He was grateful for the relief it gave him, and he also suddenly became much better at the game. His stash of dMon grew quickly, and he was thrilled when there was talk of being able to exchange some of it into BitCoins, another online currency, but one that was starting to have a value in the real world.

There were things in the TheWar game that started to worry him, but he went along with some of it and was quickly rewarded. So he ignored the alarm bells, and in the end he found that the game was unearthing long forgotten views from his youth that he hadn't thought much about for years, but now they began to resonate with his newfound vigour.

*

"How do we get across here without anyone noticing?" Nurul asked. The aim of the game that night was to slip away from their own radar so they could make an unauthorised attack on the enemy that would turn the battle and earn them a million dMons. But only if they got away with it.

"We could go under the radar. We'd disappear in ground clutter easily with those mountains." Agung looked at the terrain map on his screen.

"But we could also get shot down by a SAM. They have their own radar which will pick us up no matter what, and if we're low and fast, they'll shoot first and not even bother to ask questions later. But we could hide in plain sight. Mix with commercial traffic." Nurul was a Warrior Pilot in the game, but she was also using her real world airline pilot experience.

"How would you do that?" Agung liked a direct approach, gung-ho even, but had learnt to listen to his savvy co-pilot, both in the real cockpit and in the game.

"Well, if we choose a point of handover and then simply don't check in with the next controller. Then slip on to an airway to look like commercial traffic."

"But then a civilian controller would pick us up and want to know who we are and what we are doing."

"I don't think so. They're really only looking for secondary radar and we wouldn't be squawking. So even if they saw us on primary, they wouldn't have a level on us and probably take us for military. Maybe high or low level, but nothing to do with them. If we stay a mile or so off the airway we won't bump into anyone, but we'd still look like commercial traffic to military radar." She thought she had covered all the angles.

Agung studied the map carefully, with the familiar geographical contours overlaid by airways and airspace boundaries and special use airspace and navigation aids and waypoints and lines of latitude and longitude. It looked like the web of a deranged spider, but to Agung it was crystal clear.

"Not a bad idea, and look here. We can run parallel to the boundary from down here all the way up there and confuse them even more. Both controllers will think we're talking to the other.

"But that's not an airway."

"Doesn't matter at that point. Once they have got it into their minds we're commercial traffic, that'll just look like a direct routing. As long as we use the airways waypoints it looks like we're still under civilian control."

"And then we'll simply drop off radar out here somewhere." Nurul pointed to a position well away from land.

"Yes, radar doesn't cover much more than that. Let's try it. What'll it cost us if they nail us?"

"A fine. Maybe ten thousand dMons. No more than a hundred. Remember when we tried to attack the London Docklands? Didn't work, so they slapped us on the wrist. We could make a million on this." Nurul knew it was digital money, game money, but a million is a million and it quickened her pulse.

"Do you think there's anything in the rumours that we'll be able to convert some dMons to BitCoins soon?"

"Nah, don't think so. Anyway dMons may be worth more than BitCoins one day."

"True. Stranger things have happened. All right, let's get on with it, who are we talking to?"

*

With the cockpit voice recorder still running, Gupta doesn't say anything. Instead he unplugs his headset and holds up the jack plug for Sinna to see. It is a small gesture that will test her readiness to continue as planned. Most of the talking is behind them anyway, they each know where the other stands, but this is their first step into the void.

She looks at him calmly and reaches down and unplugs her own headset from the socket on the cockpit sidewall. Both pilots keep their headsets on even if they are now unplugged, just so the cabin crew won't notice anything unusual when they bring them refreshments a little later.

Gupta holds an index finger to his pursed lips and then points to the cockpit roof, indicating that the cockpit area microphone is still working. He then takes out a crisply folded handkerchief from his pocket and picks out three small squares of duct tape. He reaches up to the cockpit area microphone and puts the three patches over it, one over the other. Now the voice recorder is deaf, but even so they will be keeping their voices down during the rest of the flight.

"Ready?" A tiny word for such a monumental decision.

"Affirm," she replies softly. There is a little quiver in her voice, but her tone is clear and insistent.

The fact that Sinna uses brief, unambiguous aviation English now, and not just "yes," shows Gupta that this is the pilot in her who is talking. The Warrior Pilot.

"Heading 270 while I change the flight plan. Shallow banks."

Gupta reflects briefly on how different airline flying is to the aerobatics he revelled in as a young pilot. Throwing an aircraft around the sky was the perfect way to hone his handling skills and also a great way to channel those youthful impulses into something disciplined and useful. He had briefly been on the national aerobatics team before giving it up to concentrate on his airline career, and from then on his flying had been all about creating the illusion that his passengers had not left the ground. But he sometimes did aerobatics on his flight simulator and was convinced he could roll his big airliner without breaking it if need be.

"Heading 270, shallow banks."

Sinna responds just as calmly as if she were taking routine instructions. Only their muted voices betray that this is no longer an everyday flight.

She leaves the autopilot in charge of the aircraft in order to make her manoeuvres smooth and imperceptible. No rocking the boat. She selects 5 on the bank limiter, turns the heading knob to 270 degrees and switches the autopilot from navigation to heading mode. The aircraft turns left so gently that no-one on board will notice, even if they are awake.

"Confirm transponder in standby." Sinna reminds her captain of the importance that air traffic control don't spot the turn. Hopefully they won't think much of the transponder disappearing since the flight is close to the limit of their range and would soon drop off their screens anyway. Besides, Lumpur have just handed the flight over to Ho Chi Minh so the flight is no longer their concern. It is even possible that Ho Chi Minh has instructed the flight to "squawk standby" if they are having issues with their own secondary radar system.

"Confirm." Gupta rechecks the position of the switch on the transponder box between them.

"But military could pick us up on primary."

There are two kinds of radar, primary and secondary. Primary radar is a signal that is sent out from the radar antenna and reflected back from anything it hits, but this echo is weak and can disappear for a number of reasons to do with weather and terrain.

That's what secondary radar was invented for. It uses a piece of equipment on board the aircraft, called the transponder, to actively send out a radio signal in reply to a radar beam hitting it. In technical jargon that signal is called a squawk, and it is much stronger than the natural reflection and also contains the altitude of the aircraft and other flight details. That's why the captain switched it off.

"Maybe. If they're awake," Gupta replies. "But military radar aren't looking for the transponder, so they won't miss it."

"I know. Funny how little they know about civilian traffic."

"They'd be very busy if they had to look at all that. And they'd have to be tapped into information about civilian flight plans. To them it's probably just a nuisance. They're looking for things that stand out from the regular flow of traffic. Fast jets, or unusually high or low targets. Things that look like a threat."

"I guess. Our luck. But maybe we should monitor 121.5 just in case."

121.5 megahertz is the civilian aviation radio frequency but also the frequency the military would use to contact a civilian aircraft. Military aircraft communicate on the UHF radio band and civilian on the VHF band, so they normally can't talk to each other at all, except on this emergency frequency.

"OK. If they pick us up I'll say we're diverting to Pulau Langkawi with an engine problem."

"Then what?"

"We'll take it from there. I don't think it'll happen. But best get up to 360 on this heading."

In order to provide separation, aircraft operate at different altitudes, or flight levels, depending on the direction they move in. Odd numbers on easterly headings and even numbers on westerly headings.

"Up to 360." Sinna dials in flight level 360 which is a thousand feet higher than their current level and the correct level on their new, westerly heading. Then she engages Altitude

Capture and checks that the autothrottle maintains their speed in the climb.

With Sinna flying, Gupta is in charge of the navigation, and he turns his attention to his flight management computer at the top of the console. First he deletes the flight plan to Beijing. The aircraft continues unaffected because it is in heading mode. Then he takes out his mobile phone and finds the new plan hidden among contacts in his phone book.

"Wrote it down. Know I should have memorised it, but I didn't want to get it wrong. Can't see how it can hurt." Gupta's voice is a little defensive.

"Me too. I'll check them against mine when you've put them in."

Gupta enters five new waypoints into the computer:

NTW, VAS, TOSOK, MEMAK and 33°23′S–77°45′E

The first two are the identifiers of navigation aids on the east and west side of the Malaysian Peninsula. They are in the flight management system's database, so entering the identifiers will bring up their exact positions, and following them will make the aircraft look like any other traffic going about its lawful business.

The next two waypoints are just points in space on the airways system leading west across the Indian Ocean. They have been chosen because they sit on the boundary between Kuala Lumpur and Jakarta flight information regions where national airspaces meet and pilots change from one country's air traffic control system to the next. In these border regions, controllers are likely to assume, if they are not called by an aircraft in its vicinity, that it is still talking to the other country's controllers.

At waypoint MEMAK, air traffic control passes to Chennai on the east coast of India, a thousand miles away to the west. But with no radar to cover the passage of the Indian Ocean, Batam 8125 is free to turn south-west for its final waypoint.

Which is a truly terrifying one. 33 degrees, 23 minutes south and 77 degrees, 45 minutes east is not somewhere commercial aircraft ever go. It is in the middle of the Indian Ocean, with more than two thousand miles to Africa in the west, India in the north, Australia in the east and Antarctica in the south.

It is also the position of something called the Ter Tholen Fracture Zone, a place no less frightening than it sounds. There, two of Earth's tectonic plates rub against each other below thousands of feet of water, creating great mountain ranges and deep, narrow valleys.

*

When Air France flight 447 disappeared over the South Atlantic in 2009, it ended up on an underwater plain—a large expanse of flat seabed. It still took two years and tens of millions of dollars to find the black boxes and solve the mystery which turned out to be a little bit of ice on an air speed sensor. What a comeuppance to the lords of high tech. And a lesson to a few others who were listening carefully.

What they understood was that if you want to hide the wreckage of an aircraft in the sea, you need to make sure it ends up where the seabed is not flat. The mountainous Ter Tholen Fracture Zone is the perfect place to hide the wreckage of Batam 8125.

*

Sinna checks the waypoints from her own notes. She reads each named waypoint carefully and checks the details of the coordinates from right to left to avoid the danger of reading what she expects to see instead of what's actually there before her. Reading backwards, the mind doesn't know what to expect and is therefore more likely to spot errors. An old proofreader's trick that some pilots have adopted for critical data.

She confirms the flight plan, copies it across to the system on her side of the console, activates it and switches the autopilot to NAV mode. The aircraft imperceptibly adjusts its track towards the first waypoint, Narathewat or NTW for short.

Then a soft gong goes off and the flight planning computer flashes an amber message: FUEL.

They started the flight with enough fuel for their 2500 nautical mile planned route to Beijing, with extra fuel to hold for 30 minutes on arrival for bad weather or air traffic delays, more fuel for a planned diversion to another airport in case landing becomes impossible at the destination, and finally 45 minutes' reserve on top of all that.

But their new route is 3500 nautical miles long.

Gupta reaches down to his flight management system and cancels the alarm.

"We have to save some fuel. I'll see what works best."

There are several ways to fly longer on a given amount of fuel. You can fly higher, where the air is thinner, or you can slow down. It's a complex game of give and take that also involves wind and temperatures, all of which can only be precisely worked out during the actual flight. Preflight planning uses averages or forecasts, but things often work out a little differently in reality. So pilots are used to rechecking flight plans in the air, and these days the flight management computer has all the information it needs to work this out with complete accuracy. In this case deadly accuracy.

Gupta starts from the end and works backwards.

"When we flame out we'll start descending at about 3000 feet per minute to maintain airspeed. That's 12 minutes from flight level 360 which is about 80 miles. So we want to plan to run her dry 80 miles from Ter Tholen."

He deliberately uses the words "flame out" and "run dry" to check the reaction of his young co-pilot. He can't see any.

"How much leeway have we got?" She sounds like she is discussing a routine diversion. Her training kicks in and she deals with the question professionally.

"The fault line is about eighty miles long. The waypoint is in the middle, so forty miles either way."

They have been through this many times but now they are putting it into practice they need each other's reassurance.

"OK, so dry tanks at Ter Tholen minus eighty."

"Right."

Gupta punches in the numbers on his flight management system. It's not as easy as usual because the software is not designed to let pilots run the tanks dry, so he keeps getting warnings that he has to work around. He gets there in the end.

"That's 3000 nautical miles from here, and we have fuel for 2700."

"Is that with current winds?"

"Yes, we've got 32 knots from 225 degrees at the moment, but we have no forecasts further south. We'll just have to suck it and see. We could climb to flight level 400 but the wind could be stronger up there. Or stay here and reduce to Mach point eight."

At high altitudes, jet aircraft speed is measured in fractions of the speed of sound, called Mach 1. The new calculations require them to fly a little slower than they had planned for, but that's how they can stretch their fuel.

"What does that do to our ETA?"

"Plus seventeen minutes. 7 hours instead of 6 hours 43 from now. Hmm, won't make much difference at that point. What do you think?"

Sinna hesitates. She is thinking about the last part of their flight. They are due to land in Beijing at 6.40 AM local time, and the cabin crew would need to start serving breakfast at least an hour before. That means everyone will be awake at 5.30. As long as it is dark, no-one in the cabin has an inkling they are flying south-west instead of north towards Beijing. Or over open water instead of over land. But as soon as light appears on the horizon at least the cabin crew, but also some of the more attentive passengers, will realise they are going the wrong way, simply because the light is on the opposite side of the aircraft from where it should be. That will make everything more difficult, and the longer that lasts, the nastier it could all get.

"How did it look at flight level 400?"

"We could keep point eight four up there which is twenty knots more airspeed but we might have more headwind. There's not much in it."

"I agree," she finally says.

"OK, set point eight."

Sinna reaches up and sets .80 in the autopilot speed select window on the cockpit coaming. That's 0.8 times the speed of sound at their altitude of 36000 feet. The autothrottle system moves the power levers back slightly, and the airspeed indicator slowly unwinds a fraction. She listens for a change in engine note. Cabin crew know what to expect of a normal flight and might react to an unexpected change of engine sound in the middle of a long flight, if only to check if there's anything they should know or do. But the change is so subtle and gradual she can't hear it.

*

Forty minutes later, Batam 8125 is approaching waypoint TOSOK just north of Sumatra, and no-one seems to have detected them on their new route. Or if anyone has, they have assumed it was someone else's responsibility, rather than cause a fuss that may mean waking up a superior at two in the morning. That was the plan, and it seems to work.

At TOSOK their new routing takes them along the boundaries between the airspaces of Malaysia, Sumatra and India for their next waypoint, MEMAK. This conveniently takes them further and further away from land and therefore radar cover and also has a good chance of convincing anyone who might see them on radar that they are someone else's problem.

But they are not entirely out of the woods yet, even if the last half hour seems to have confirmed the idea that an entire airliner can be made to disappear with the use of a few simple tricks and careful timing.

Down below, in a bunker on the Royal Malaysian Air Force Butterworth airbase, the night watch is into its second hour. The lone radar operator follows procedure, but that doesn't take up much of his time. For the rest, the game he is playing on his smartphone is a lot more interesting than watching the few faint echoes from commercial airliners that are crossing his screen at a snail's pace. On the phone things are not only more colourful and exciting, and move a good deal faster, but he's not a controller any more. He's a pilot, an active participant; he can be a hero if he wants to.

He does check his radar screen from time to time, but there is nothing on it he hasn't seen before. Boring, boring, boring airliners coming and going, and not very many of them this time of night. OK, maybe one of them is on a slightly unusual route, but commercial pilots under pressure to save time and fuel are requesting, and getting, more and more direct routings nowadays, instead of following the wanderings of the airways. That's probably all it is. Nothing to get excited about, and certainly nothing to do anything about.

*

The soft chime that indicates a call from the cabin goes off. Captain Gupta picks up the handset from the cradle on the console.

"Yeah, helloo." He makes it as casual as he can.

"Bashini here, Captain. Anything you need up there?" asks the chief purser.

"No thanks, we're fine for the moment."

"OK, talk to you in a bit," comes back the reply. Cabin crew check on the flight deck two to three times an hour, partly to check if they need anything from the galley, but also as a safety measure.

"Coming up to MEMAK." Gupta reminds his co-pilot that their last turn is approaching.

"Roger. We're still in shallow bank mode, so nobody'll notice."

Most of the passengers are asleep now, but there is always a nervous flier who isn't, and at least some of the cabin crew should be awake. It's important they don't feel the changes of direction.

A few minutes later the aircraft makes its gentle turn onto the last leg towards Ter Tholen, a straight run of 2500 nautical miles to the south-west.

"Five forty-five to go. That's an ETA of zero two five Zulu."

Gupta works time in UTC, or GMT as it was before space travel caused it to be extended to the whole universe, referred to as "Z" or Zulu in aviation. On international flights, pilots can't constantly adjust for local time as they cross time zones flying east or west, so they use the time at the international time line in Greenwich, London instead.

That gets a bit confusing when operating far away from it, but the benefit is that it stays constant. Singapore and Chinese local times are both eight hours ahead of UTC, so 25 minutes past midnight Zulu is 8.25 AM local time.

But expected arrival time in Beijing is 6.30. Singapore—and Chinese—time.

"They'll know for two hours." A shiver runs through her.

"We've got a good story to tell them."

"We shouldn't adjust…" she searches for the right word "touchdown instead?"

"Can't have any fuel left on impact. That would leave an oil slick that's visible from satellites. But more important we have to go all the way to Ter Tholen. Seabed's too flat further north. This flight has got to vanish with no trace. Don't lose your nerve now, we've got all this planned. It's worked fine so far, it'll work the rest of the way."

Gupta is convincing himself as much as his young co-pilot. He reaches across the console, for the first time on the flight, and takes her hand. It shakes slightly, or maybe it's his own.

"We'll be fine, you'll see. We're doing the right thing," he says softly as they continue their race into the night.

7. THE CABIN

Everyone is strapped in for takeoff, and cabin crew have switched the doors to automatic. This little ritual means that the long slides built into the doors for emergency evacuation will be released and inflated automatically if the doors are opened. That's for safety should there be a need to get everyone out quickly. They must be able to do so in ninety seconds, and under that pressure the procedure has to be as simple as possible. Therefore "Doors to automatic" before departure, and back to Manual before being opened in normal circumstances, or else there will be a lot of red faces, and possible worse, injuries. Hence the elaborate ritual of crosschecks round the doors before takeoff and landing.

William can see the two middle doors from his seat in row 30 and shakes his head inwardly. He is no engineer and all he knows about planes is what he has gleaned on reasonably frequent flights on the West Coast 'bus' route between LA and 'Frisco, but he doesn't understand why this small part of flying hasn't been automated long ago.

The big jet moves over the tarmac with soft bumps while passengers check out their home for the next six hours. There are seat pockets with strange contents to be explored, and touch screens in front of everyone that look like a coarser, paler version of their own computer pads. Many prepare for sleep, take off shoes and make themselves comfortable so they can nod off as soon as they are airborne, but others are more apprehensive and don't want to do anything the gods could take as a challenge, such as assuming that the big aircraft will ever leave the ground.

Or get back on it for that matter. A lot offer up silent prayers, and a few believe that's all that will keep them alive for the next few hours.

Then the two big jet engines start their soft roar. Farah squeezes Hamizan's hand a little tighter, and her dark brown eyes seek reassurance from her husband. He smiles at her and in that moment, maybe for the first time, he realises how much she loves him. It's the way she looks at him. The way she touches him.

As the aircraft picks up speed, Ariel Beckman reaches for his champagne glass that has started sliding back on the side tray. The bumps from the nose wheel speed up and up and up and then suddenly stop as the nose of the aircraft rises into the air. A few seconds later it is as if all motion stops. They are airborne. The final act is the noise from the gear doors opening into the airstream, a little louder than the engines far behind him, and the clonk and the silence as the big gear stows away inside the plane's body. He always gets a deeply sensual pleasure from following that sequence, and he's glad people don't know how he finds the whole process of taking off in a big aircraft strangely sexual, especially when sitting this far up front. He is sure nobody else feels like that.

Half an hour later Yan is fast asleep, as are her mother and grandmother and most others in tourist class. There is no meal service in the back until the morning on this night flight to Beijing. William tries to doze, but even with the little bit of extra leg room in the front row, he can't get comfortable enough to sleep. Oh well, maybe there's something interesting on the inflight entertainment system.

In the front cabin, Farah and Hamizan are well into what is one of the finest meals they have ever tasted. The menus came in heavily embossed covers as in the grandest restaurants and, while they were not as long, the contents were impressive. Three starters, three main courses, including a vegetarian choice, and two desserts. Farah selects the vegetarian main course, not because she is vegetarian, but because it sounds tempting. And because she wants to keep her looks for Hamizan, and she might as well start now. She is well aware how some men's eyes start roving surprisingly soon after their wedding. The wine list also looks imposing, but they have no need for it. Neither of them has ever touched a drop of alcohol.

Farah is thinking what a meal like that would cost in a fine restaurant. She only has a vague idea because she has never been to such a place, and she doesn't want to ask Hamizan. It's another of her bubbles, bright and shining and fragile, and it will burst as soap bubbles burst when you try to catch them if she asks about money or anything to do with the real world. So she puts her bubble away inside her where its soft shimmer will be safe for as long as she lives.

In the seat in front, Ariel Beckman savours the aroma of the Sassicaia in his glass and watches the heavy curtains of dark red wine forming on the inside of the glass when he swirls it gently. He has hardly tasted it yet and is torn between the pleasure of his eyes and nose and that of his palate. Anyway, he knows that most of the pleasure of wine is in the nose. How the blazes do they get this stuff these days? He can't get it for love or money any more. Well, that's not strictly true; he saw it recently at five hundred Aussie dollars a bottle, but that's too steep even for him. He realises he is having a two hundred and fifty dollar bottle of wine with his airline meal, and could probably get another if he asked. Business class indeed.

In the midst of all this, no-one on board notices that the aircraft diverts from its northeasterly track towards Beijing and takes up a westerly course across the Malaysian Peninsula. The blinds are down all the way round the cabin to prevent light disturbing the pilots should they enter cloud, which is not likely at this altitude, but putting the blinds down at night is standard procedure whatever the flight. It also stops the flashing strobes on the wingtips disturbing sleeping passengers, or setting off seizures in sensitive people. There are so many obscure little details in aviation, it's a wonder how all of it ever comes together.

*

The first to look for the early light of dawn is probably Chief Purser Faisal Bashini. It is one of the small pleasures he gets from these night flights. A couple of hundred quietly sleeping passengers is a big bonus and does reduce the workload, but even if it is lighter work, long night flights are hard on the body. He is getting to an age where he can feel that; not so much on the flights but the day after when he can't find sleep as he used to, at any time of the day.

He has started preparing for the morning meal—cold sandwiches in the back and a choice of English or Continental up front. Including the inevitable requests for soft boiled eggs which are so difficult to get right, up here with a cabin altitude of eight thousand feet where water boils at 92 Centigrade or 198 Fahrenheit. He could kill the buggers who send them back if they are not spot on. Funnily enough that's always men. Maybe because they never boil their own.

Only trouble is, there is nothing to see when he first looks out the window on the right side of the galley. It's coming up to 5.20 AM, and there should be the faintest trace of light in the east. Maybe the mist is still with them; that can block out the birth of the dawn, and he is always disappointed when it does, so he keeps looking when his work allows.

The galley ovens have heated up and are starting to send out their enticing morning smells. The coffee makers are bubbling, adding to the aroma and waking people up to the new day. Faisal always jokes that somebody should build an alarm clock that does that; they would make a fortune.

"Faisal." Senior air hostess Kya Chanda is in charge in the aft galley but now puts her head round the corner of the forward galley where Bashini is working this morning.

"Yes?" He is surprised to see her at this busy time. More than 200 mouths to feed, and less than hour to do it in. "Everything all right?"

"I don't know. It's just that it should be getting light by now. A couple of regular passengers on this route have been asking why it's not. We've been thinking the same thing." He can hear she has been discussing it with her colleagues in the back of the aircraft.

"It should start getting light out to the east when we start the breakfast service. It did on my last flight a week ago. When did you last check with the flight deck?" She looks to him for an explanation that's not the catastrophe she has started to fear.

"Twenty minutes ago, just before I started preparing for breakfast. Brought them coffee, everything was fine. It's probably just the haze." But her question adds to his own doubts and he hears the hollow ring of his answer. The sun doesn't jump around the sky at random. It's reliable and predictable, it's the heartbeat of time itself. Haze can blot out the dawn for a short while, but not hold it back for long. Heavy clouds can do that, but there should be none of those at cruising altitude this time of year, and if there were they would have felt the turbulence.

He suddenly gets an icy feeling that something is very wrong. He can't put his finger on what it is, but he can't ignore it any longer.

"I'll check with the flight deck," he says and makes for the interphone handset above the crew seat by the forward door. What the hell is going on?

8. THE WAR GAME

I did feel all the things Omar was talking about. I felt them very strongly, and now he was forcing me to put up or shut up. Or maybe simply to grow up.

I looked into his eyes for something I could object to, argue with. Hatred. Or despair. Or greed. What I saw was mostly pain, but there was something else which I hadn't seen in him for a long time. I recognised the glimmer of a dream, or at least the hope of one. The man I loved was starting to come alive again, and I knew better than to crush that hope. It would be crueller than what that filthy copper had done to him.

I didn't know what I was letting myself in for but I it was suddenly clear to me that I had no choice if I ever wanted to look myself in the eye again. I had been freewheeling through life with youthful talk for long enough. Now I needed to start pulling my weight.

"OK Ome, tell me about it."

"Really?"

"Yes, really. I want to be with you all the way. I'm not sure I believe we can do it, but if there's any chance we can use TheWar as a tool to make the world a better place, we should do it. I still think it's pompous to think that we can, but I also think we have a duty to try. We have close to a hundred million users now. If we aren't going to turn that into money, we should do something else with it." For once I let myself talk before thinking, but I believed my own words as soon as I heard them come out of my mouth.

"That's what I've been thinking," Omar replied eagerly. "Apart from the users, we already have most of the tools we need. Lots of different games and lots of different kinds of warriors, and we can create more as we need them. Pilot Warrior is one of the most popular groups, last I looked we had nearly four million of them. We need to find out how many are real pilots and then start selecting the ones that we can groom. Same for other specialists. People in finance, train drivers, power plant engineers, things like that."

"We need to do some serious psychological profiling as well. We already have some, but we need to do it for real."

"Exactly. We need help with that. We also need more help with the pilots. We already have instructors, but we've got to move on to a completely different level, still making sure it looks like the same game. We can't recruit in the real world, far too risky. It's got to be completely within the parameters of the game so if anyone gets nosy we can stare at them with our big, blue eyes and say don't be an idiot, this is just a computer game. Then we slowly move players with the right skills and attitudes closer and closer to reality. That way there's a good chance we can pick the few handfuls of real warriors we need from nearly a hundred million candidates. People who already want to change things, people who are fed up with the status quo. People like ourselves but with the skills we need. Pilots and engineers and bankers. Maybe even coppers or soldiers, or come of the civilian contractors who work for them."

"So where do we start?"

"Maybe with the profiling? We could base it on the info they give us, but we could also start analysing the way they play—what they do and how they do it. Find those who bend the rules and thrive on risk. Then whittle those down to people with real grievances or strong convictions. And by cross-referencing with what people say about each other. Didn't we have some help setting up the profiling we already have?"

"Yes, it was the first shrink you went to. The idea was to help you back on your feet by getting you back to work. It was just after your operation and you were totally not interested so it didn't work out, but she didn't know that. I used all the stuff she gave you and coded it myself. But maybe we could go back and say that you are getting back on your feet now and you've had this great new idea and could she help you work it out?"

"Trouble is that the details we have on players could be entirely fictitious. Most of them probably are."

"Yes, so we need to give people an incentive to post real data."

"We could bribe them. With dMons or with privileges."

"Way to go." I was beginning to see a structure to his idea.

"But we'll need to explain why, and I've been thinking the best strategy might be to tell the truth. Or as near as dammit."

"How do you mean?"

"We could create new versions of all the games, more 'real' versions. Virtual reality reality."

"Double bluff."

"You could call it that. We'd be installing more mirrors in our hall of mirrors. It'll move us closer to reality and at the same time make everything impossible to see through. Reality? Of course it's real. Within the framework of the virtual reality within the game called TheWar. Really for real? What have you been smoking?"

"And then, when it becomes really real?"

"We can either hide it in plain sight or send it so deep underground nobody'll ever find it. We'll decide later."

"But there's got to come a point when the player realises this is not a game any more."

"Yes, the moment of truth. We've got to be careful about that. We can't let anyone get near that point without being absolutely sure they're committed. We'll have to work on the details, but it's got to be based on the psychological profiling, and we should also collect as much dirt on those guys as possible so we have a hold on them if necessary. Which I hope it won't be. It'll be much better to work with willing volunteers, so that's how we should design the whole thing. We can't force anyone to do anything but just have to let those with the right natural instincts reveal themselves and then encourage and train them. Carrots, not sticks. All the guys who go to Taliban training camps don't do so at gunpoint. They go there of their own free will, even pay to get there, because they already want to. All we have to do is find the same kind of guys among our players."

*

The first part of our plan worked like a dream, and the National Health Service, bless them, gladly provided free expert help to design a profiling system for our warriors. I couldn't believe how gullible they were.

"I want to start working full time again," Omar told his new psychologist once he had arranged a series of sessions with her.

"This was the idea last year, but I wasn't ready then. I am now. What I want to do is make the internet game that my partner and I run more realistic, and to do that we need to improve the psychological profiling of our players so they get more out of the game. If you can give me some help with the things we should be looking for, that would really get me going."

He obviously didn't tell her that we knew how to squeeze data like that for every last drop of blood. It was important not to spook her but to let her believe firmly she was just helping her psychologically damaged patient to get back on the horse.

She ended up designing a very complex set of values for each player, detailing everything we could possibly hope to find out about them: ethnicity and sexuality, eating habits and taste in music, education and jobs, religious and political beliefs, and levels of aggression, frustration and fulfilment. Plus everything in between.

Then we took over and designed ways to collect all this material automatically, both from what the players volunteered and from the way they played the games and the information they gave away there, bit by bit, often without realising. We double-checked everything as much as we could and cross-checked with other players. In the end what players said about each other turned up some of the most useful data.

Omar and I knew from our work with large customer databases both how to collect data covertly and how to make sense of vast amounts of raw data once it was collected. Supermarkets and online companies turn the behaviour of their customers into incredibly sophisticated and subtle ways of manipulating them.

The days of merely analysing people's shopping for their likes and dislikes and making sure the right amounts of the right goods are on the shelves at the right time are long gone. Shops and web sites are now designed to guide, or beguile, customers into buying things they wouldn't otherwise have bought, or maybe bought somewhere else. Much of this information is traded among companies and is gradually seeping into every aspect of our lives. Your bank knows you need a loan or mortgage long before you have decided to buy a car or a home, online traders tell you what you want before you think of it and targeted advertising is being sent to your computer screen or smartphone based on deeply personal clues you leave behind all the time. Programmers like us are the ones who are pulling the strings and harvesting all that knowledge.

We used all the tricks of the trade to mine our player profiles for the information we wanted, and the results were staggering. Very soon we had separated out a small minority of players, fewer than one in a thousand, but still tens of thousands of people, with high aggression levels, low fulfilment levels and some kind of extremist views, political or religious. Most of those had to be discarded as useless for one reason or another, but it still left several thousand players with the skills, jobs, attitudes and aptitudes we needed.

The first step in the plan had succeeded beyond our craziest imaginings. Now we needed to find a way to exploit the opportunities and vulnerabilities we had uncovered.

And go to war.

9. THE FLIGHT DECK

"Well, you may believe you are doing the right thing," Nurul Sinna is thinking. "But I do it because I don't have a choice. All right, I agree with the aim but no way in hell would I kill myself, or anybody else, for a cause—any cause—unless somebody had me by the very short and curlies."

*

But they did. She had been horrified when she found out how Gupta had let himself be influenced, brainwashed she thought, into planning the disappearance of an airliner in the name of some global fight against capitalism. At first she tried to talk him out of it, but he was determined to see the plan through. It was put together using many of the elements they had practised while playing TheWar games, but the mad thought that all that was done in order to groom players to do the same in the real world was so far-fetched it had never entered her mind.

It occurred to her that nobody had thought of people flying airliners into skyscrapers either, until suddenly somebody did it. She had been as naïve as everybody else, but that was little consolation. When she fully realised what was happening, and that she couldn't stop her senior colleague from going through with it, she had threatened to alert the airline or go to the authorities.

"I won't do it, Agung," she had pleaded forcefully when it finally dawned on her that her captain was serious. "I *can't* do it. And I won't let you do it either. Don't you see how crazy it is? I'll

93

stop it, I'll go to the Chief Pilot, or to the police, or the press. I don't know who, but I'll stop it."

"If you do, the Warlords will destroy you," Gupta had told her. "They know all about how you slept your way to your job, with whom, where, every detail of how, how often and especially why." Gupta felt the shame burn within him as he lashed his lover with things he had so enjoyed himself, but he was unable to stop. "They say you got some of your qualifications that way, or at least eased them along. I don't know if that's true, or any of the details, they just told me to tell you that they'll tell everyone. Including your family, especially your family, and your entire village. It'll break your parents, probably kill them. And bring down a lot of others besides."

"It'll kill my parents if I disappear into thin air," she had argued.

"Maybe, but they won't die disgraced. Nor will you."

She knew she had only herself to thank for being in this impossible position. She had known the effect she had on men from a very young age, and to begin with it was all so innocent. A sweet smile, a demure flash of her brown eyes, and many men got that lost look, the one that said they wanted more, much more. Of course she didn't know what they wanted until years later, but she found out early that many things came easier to her when she used her little charms.

By the time she was twelve she knew exactly what boys wanted, and men. Not that any of them got it, but she had allowed them a look, and even a touch. She had seen the fire in their eyes, now and again even madness for the forbidden fruit, and she had been a little afraid sometimes, but she quickly learned to control her admirers through their own fear. And she learned to use it to get what she wanted, in the sweetest possible way.

A couple of years later it was no holds barred as Nurul embarked on a real career of turning men's heads. Not that she became what people consider a prostitute, but that was mostly because she was so careful to keep her air of innocence that nobody would have believed what she was up to. That innocence added to her allure, so it worked both to protect her reputation and to make many men weak at the knees.

Of course there was never any question of payment, but when she found out how much she could improve her grades with a few simple favours, she homed in on her male teachers. She had to be careful around them, because she knew she would suffer as much as they if anyone found out, so she kept perfecting her little-girl act, and only the few who were up to their necks in it had any inkling of what really went on.

It was one of her man friends who took her flying for the first time as a way to impress her, and she loved it immediately. He owned a small two-seater aircraft and showed her how to move the controls to make it do what she wanted. Manipulating things to get a desired effect was something she understood well, and she was a fast learner.

The first time Nurul did a loop was when she had her first orgasm. She only realised what was happening because she had found out about orgasms in order to feign them, but when a real one came it gushed through her like a waterfall. Flying was the sexiest thing she had done in her entire life, in fact the only thing that had ever really turned her on, and no-one was going to keep her away from it. When she left school she set about that plan with the same determination that had secured her position as top of her class. .

By then it had become second nature to use her effect on men to her advantage, but she realised that she had to work hard if she wanted to become any good as a pilot. Her charms might move things along and get her a little faster past some of the most boring goal posts, but there was no substitute for doing the work. But this was something she wanted, so for the first time in her life she put in the effort that was expected, and she found out how easy it was when she did something she loved and had a talent for.

Still, she advanced quicker than her contemporaries, but few thought to question that. She advanced purely on merit, or so it seemed. But that was only part of the truth, and although she had become an outstanding pilot, the way she had gone about it would destroy her career if it came out.

She knew she shouldn't have done it, she knew that she could have got where she was without it, and she knew that she shouldn't have trusted others to keep quiet about it. First and foremost she should have known better than to expose herself in that idiotic computer game, but it was too late to change any of that now.

*

Her only option is to outwit both her captain and his puppet masters, without getting caught in the middle. Which is why she finds herself at the controls of an airliner with 233 people on board who trust her blindly to take them safely to Beijing, and what she has done so far is take them more than 2000 miles away from where they should have been. But she has been working on a plan to make up for that.

She has carefully calculated and memorised all the distances and timings on their suicidal route into the southern Indian Ocean, and she need not refer to any notes. If she can get control of the flight deck some time in the next hour and a half, she will still have enough fuel to return to either Singapore or Jakarta. Even an hour later, she could make it to Cocos Island, about halfway back towards Indonesia. Its runway is a little short, but the aircraft would be almost out of fuel by then, and therefore very light, so she knows she wouldn't have a problem landing.

Any time after that would be too late and she wouldn't have enough fuel to make it to an airport. Heading for anywhere in Australia would only make her crash into the ocean in a different place than the one decided by the Warlords, but crash nonetheless. That might make any wreckage more likely to be found, but she wants to save herself and everyone else, not just make the job of the accident investigators easier.

The key to her plan is for her to end up the hero. If she manages to take control and return the aircraft and everyone in it safely, Gupta and the Warlords can say what they want about her. No-one will believe them.

She has made dozens of plans for taking over the cockpit and rejected nearly all of them as unworkable or too risky. She needs to find a way to make Gupta leave the flight deck so she can take over. But even if she can, there is a risk that he will turn the tables on her and convince the others that she is the hijacker bent on killing them all and somehow take back control.

The best plan she has come up with is that she should leave the flight deck and convince the cabin crew that they are all headed for destruction, and then get them to help her overpower the captain. But she knows it won't be easy to get away from the flight deck, and it may be just as difficult to convince her colleagues in the back.

With time ticking by, she decides to make her move.

"I've got to take a comfort break," she says.

"No way. I don't want you back in the cabin now," Gupta replies.

"Why not? They can't have noticed anything yet. Or if they have, it'll be a chance to calm them down. If anything was wrong, the last thing one of us would do is appear in the cabin, don't you see that?" She hoped she didn't sound as tense as she felt.

"I don't care. It's too risky. Do what you have to do where you are."

Sinna is taken aback. It is something she had not thought of, but the disgusting suggestion makes her react with genuine outrage.

"You've got to be kidding. You want me to sit here for three more hours in my own excrement? You want to sit next to that?" Her face is red with fury.

Gupta studies her face intensely. Her threat to sell him out still rings in his ears and he is not sure he can trust her on her own, even with the threat she is under. She might have come along this far, but is she willing to go the distance? He is not sure.

"I'm here. Why would I back out now?" she says. "If that's what I wanted I'd have done it before the flight. I could have called in sick or smashed my car into something on the way to the airport. I could have done any number of things to avoid being here, but here I am."

"You know what would have happened if you did."

"And that won't happen if I back out now? Agung, you're a great fuck, but honestly, you're not the brightest guy I've slept with." She knows he is defensive about his intelligence and feels inferior to her. Backing him into a corner on that point, while tickling his manly vanity, is her best move. "It's plain as daylight that if I don't play ball, the fucking Warlords will rip me apart in front of the whole world, and I won't do that to my parents. I'm here. I'll do it, but I need a shit."

Gupta has never heard Sinna use words like that before, but now she deliberately chooses coarse language to shock her opponent and beat him into submission.

"OK, calm down. I didn't know that was it, I thought you just needed a pee. Didn't you cut down on eating as they told us?"

They had been instructed to eat nothing and drink little in the 24 hours before this flight and get by on glucose tablets and small amounts of energy drinks in order to reduce bodily waste, precisely for this reason.

"Of course I did, but I still need to go. I don't know about you but my stomach is turning. I'm not used to this martyr stuff," she adds with biting sarcasm. There's nothing wrong with her stomach, but it is the strongest excuse to leave the flight deck she can think of.

99

"OK, but use the forward lav and try to avoid contact with anyone. I want you back here quickly."

"Stop worrying, but let me go before this turns into an accident."

"Yeah, all right, I'm sorry. Go get it over with."

Sinna inches out of her seat and takes the few steps to the armoured door that separates the flight deck from the cabin. Before she opens it, she pauses and puts on her jacket and cap. Company policy calls for pilots to wear full uniform in the cabin to underline their authority, and she knows Gupta is watching. If she goes into the cabin in her shirt sleeves, he'll know she is fleeing.

10. THE CABIN

Sinna rushes past the forward lavatory in the crew rest area behind the flight deck as if running from the scene of a crime. In fact, as she sees it, she is now on a course to prevent a crime, even if she is also involved in committing it.

When she draws the curtain to the business class cabin aside, she sees Chief Purser Bashini lift the handset by the forward passenger door and realises he could be about to call the flight deck. She doesn't want Gupta to know that she has gone straight into the cabin so she has to stop that call.

Just as he is touching the flight deck button on the handset, Bashini sees the first officer come rushing through the curtain with every sign of alarm. He freezes when he sees her draw her hand quickly across her throat in a gesture that most people understand as "stop whatever you are doing, RIGHT NOW."

Bashini slowly replaces the handset in the cradle and makes a sideways nod towards the galley on his right. Sinna nods in confirmation and both crew members quickly look round the cabin to see if anyone noticed the little scene. Everyone seems to be fast asleep.

Sinna moves quickly up the aisle and turns into the galley, closing the curtains behind her.

"Hush, keep your voice down," is the first thing she says to Bashini.

"What's up? You look like you've seen a ghost." The Chief Purser senses the gravity of the situation but tries to keep a growing panic out of his voice.

"Faisal, I have something to tell you that is very hard to believe, but I need you to listen very carefully."

"OK, go ahead."

"We are not on the way to Beijing. We are headed into the Indian Ocean and the captain is going to ditch the aircraft and kill everyone in it."

At first Bashini doesn't understand what she is saying. It is so grotesquely outside anything he expected, or has ever experienced, that she might as well have been speaking Chinese.

"Come again?" is all he can think to say. But as her words start filtering through his incredulity and register in his brain, he realises that what the first officer is telling him ties in with his worries about the sunrise that hasn't appeared as expected. A wave of nausea washes over him; this is much worse than he feared.

"We're heading south, not north. If you look out the window, you'll see it starting to get light on the port side. It should be starboard if we were headed north."

Bashini cracks open the galley curtains and bends down to line up the entry door porthole with the horizon. He can now clearly see the early dawn—on the wrong side of the aircraft.

"Fucking hell, what have you done?" are his first words.

"Shsh, keep it down, we don't want the whole cabin in on this," Sinna hisses.

Bashini bites back a violent outburst and lowers his voice, but his fury is still obvious.

"The cabin! They are about to wake up, all of them, and they all know the difference between left and right. We'll have a riot on our hands in less than half an hour."

"Not if you help me."

"Help you do what? How do I know this is not something you have done? It must have been. You can't fly in the wrong direction for hours without knowing."

"Gupta threatened me. I knew but I couldn't do anything about it."

"How did you get away from him then?"

"It's complicated," she starts explaining. "He thinks he has threatened me enough to be in on it, so he let me go to the ladies'."

*

Ariel Beckman doesn't sleep well when flying, and even in his fully reclining seat he is watching the dim cabin through half closed eyes when suddenly a female pilot in full uniform pulls the curtains at the front of the cabin and stares in alarm at something behind him in the opposite aisle. She then moves her hand across her throat, apparently to stop someone doing something, and rushes down the aisle with an air of panic.

Beckman is a seasoned flyer and has never seen anything like it. He knows there's something very wrong, not least because that gesture has a very specific meaning in what used to be his profession, before he went into waste management. It's a sign to kill.

Thirty years earlier, Ariel Beckman had been a lean and mean soldier in Australia's Special Air Services Regiment, the SASR. It was a regiment with a celebrated record in conflicts like Vietnam, but in his time it had not been posted abroad. Nonetheless its members were trained to a fine pitch and were ready at all times to infiltrate and eliminate any opposition target they might be given, anywhere in the world. They could operate from virtually any aircraft, boat or vehicle and jump, swim, climb, run, walk or crawl into any position and infiltrate, observe or kill, then retreat leaving barely their footprints. Stealth is the hallmark of an SASR soldier, and although it is a long time ago, the burly businessman can still do most of it.

As soon as he hears the swish of the curtains closing behind him, he silently rolls out of his reclined seat onto the aisle. He listens for any movement indicating anyone noticing, but the only sound is soft snoring. The young couple behind him are curled up together under their blankets and are soundly asleep, and the middle row next to them is unoccupied. He stays low as he moves past those seats and close to the curtains on the right hand side of the galley, opposite where the two crew entered.

The conversation he overhears is low and intense, but then suddenly punctuated by a "Fucking hell, what have you done?" The upshot, as far as he can make out, is that they are not on the way to Beijing as they should be but flying south into the wilderness of the Indian Ocean like lambs to the slaughter.

He listens for a while longer until he is sure this is something he needs to get involved in.

*

Sinna and Bashini jerk back from their huddled conversation when the big man suddenly appears in the galley. They haven't heard him coming; one second he just appears out of nowhere.

"I'm sorry, didn't mean to startle you, but I heard what you have been saying," he says quietly. "I'm Ariel Beckman, I'm a passenger, but I'm also an ex-special forces soldier. I'm trained to deal with emergencies. It sounds like you need some help."

Bashini eyes the large man and thinks his presence can only make the situation worse.

"Please Sir, go back to your seat. The crew are dealing with this situation."

"Do you have an air marshal on board?" inquires Beckman.

"No, we don't, but the crew are fully qualified to deal with this," Bashini snaps back.

"Which one of you has crisis management training?" Beckman asks calmly. "And hostage negotiator training? And which one of you can use force effectively if it comes to that?" He looks at their blank faces. "I thought not. I say we pool our resources, and the way I read it, you are in charge here, Ma'am." He turns to Sinna.

"How do we know you are what you say you are and not just some crank?" she asks.

"I don't carry credentials, I'm a businessman these days. But not many people wear this." He pulls back his sleeve to reveal the winged dagger of the SASR tattooed on the inside of his right arm.

"All right, but even so, how can you help?"

"I'll know that when I know the situation. Please tell me what's going on, Ma'am." Ex-sergeant Beckman easily slides into military ranking and addresses the pilot as his superior officer, while using his training to calm and control the situation.

Sinna realises that this hulk of a man could be just what she needs to seize control from Gupta. She'll have to be careful how she handles him though, because she senses he will see through her story if she makes a slip. She wants to save the flight, but she, not some has-been glory boy, needs to come out the hero, or she'd be better off going through with Gupta's plan. She can't decide if she should use her charms on the Australian. If he is as good as he says he is, he would sniff her out and it would blow up in her face. She decides to play it straight with a sanitised version of the truth that she thinks she can get away with.

"The captain has flown us off course. We are headed for a remote part of the Indian Ocean and he is going to crash the aircraft and kill everyone in it. It's all to do with a complicated terrorist plot to stop people flying and put pressure on the financial systems, but that's not important now. What's important is that if I can get control of the flight deck in the next hour or so, we will still have fuel to return to either Jakarta or Cocos Island. After that it's too late and we'll crash whatever happens."

"How did the captain do all that with you in the cockpit?" Beckman asks thoughtfully.

"He has a personal hold on me. He forced me to go along with it, but I have been planning all the time to do what I am trying to do now."

Beckman ponders her reply. He senses there is something wrong with it, but on the other hand the idea that *she* is a would-be terrorist trying to take over control using help from the cabin is just too fantastic. All the same, he might as well spit it out and see how she reacts.

"It could be the other way around. It could be you trying to mutiny and take control away from the captain with the help of people from the cabin."

"Then why hasn't he turned the aircraft round yet, now that I'm not there? Or called through to the cabin to alert someone? Look out the window, the sun rises to the east, so we are flying south, not north."

Beckman decides to believe her, at least for now.

"OK Ma'am, what you say makes sense. So what do you suggest we do?"

"I need to get back to the flight deck, and the captain needs to be... disabled. I don't know how, you're the expert. You can forget about negotiating with him. Even if we had the time, he wouldn't change his mind now. He's way past the point of no return."

"What do you base that on?"

"On how hard I have tried to persuade him, and for how long. And on the fact that you haven't got a lot of time to negotiate in. But couldn't you enter behind me when I go back there and restrain him somehow?"

"The captain will be sitting in his seat? On the left hand side of the cockpit?"

"Yes."

"How far is it from the door to his seat?"

"Just a couple of steps."

"How high and wide is the seat back?"

"They are big seats. Probably nearly thirty inches wide, and including the headrest it's about level with the top of his head."

"That means it's very hard to restrain him from behind that seat. What can he do to fight me if I'm standing behind him?"

"He could make a sharp dive. If you're not strapped in, you'll go weightless and probably knock yourself out on the overhead panel. You'll have no control whatsoever. I doubt I'll have time to strap in, so I won't be any use. In fact, we could both be knocked out of action."

That's more or less what Beckman's training tells him to expect, but that was a long time ago and he needs to bring his knowledge up to date, and also probe deeper into where Sinna stands. Will she lie or tell the truth? He constantly crosschecks what she tells him and looks for inconsistencies.

"He'd need his hands and arms to do that, wouldn't he?"

"Yes, but even if you hold those, he still has his feet."

"What could he do with his feet?"

"He could kick the rudder so violently the tail breaks off. It's happened to airliners by accident before."

"And if the tail breaks off?"

"We all die. Without the tail we go into a nosedive immediately. It may be what he wants to do anyway, only much later. He wants us to get so far away no-one will ever find us, but if it's his only option he'll probably do it here and now."

She nearly adds "It's what I would do," but checks herself. She doesn't want to sow more doubt about herself than there already is.

"Too risky then. What else can we do?"

"Can't you knock him out?"

"Not if his head is protected by a big headrest. At least I couldn't be sure to do it quickly, and if he can send me flying with one push on the controls, I wouldn't have much of a chance."

"I thought you Special Forces types could kill with your bare hands in the blink of an eye," she says and doesn't quite manage to keep her little girl voice out of it.

"I can, Ma'am," Beckman replies coldly, aware that this sensuous woman is trying to work him. He does feel her feminine magnetism, in a strange way enhanced by the incongruous masculinity of her uniform, but she is his daughter's age and he is too battle-hardened to fall for it anyway.

"In several different ways," he adds just to rub it in. "But I'm not going to kill a man on your say-so. I'll restrain and render him harmless, but I won't kill him."

"But he is going to kill all of us."

"So you say."

They stare at each other for a while, and Sinna realises she's up against one of those men she can't twist around her little finger.

"Listen, this is not getting us anywhere," Bashini breaks the impasse. "Couldn't we get the captain away from the flight deck? Create some emergency that requires his presence in the cabin?"

"And then overpower him?"

"Yes. You could do that in the cabin, couldn't you?"

"Yes, easily. What do you suggest?" Beckman's attitude to the Chief Purser is less deferential than to the first officer, but at least he is not suspicious of him and he knows better than to ignore ideas from people who know things he doesn't.

"A cabin fire. Or passenger illness maybe," Bashini doesn't sound convinced himself.

"A cabin disturbance!" Sinna is eager to get back in Beckman's good graces. "He'd send me to attend to a fire, and especially a sick passenger. But he wouldn't send me to break up a fight."

"But would he go himself? Why should he be bothered about a fight if he's going to kill everyone anyway?"

"When I come back to the flight deck I'll go through the details of the rest of the flight with him. He's done that several times already, it calms him down, and it'll convince him that I'm with him all the way." Sinna turns to Bashini. "Give me fifteen minutes, I don't want him to connect the call with my having been back here. But then call him and report that a fight has broken out in the back. You thought you had it under control, but it's flaring up again and it needs the captain's authority to cool things down.

Bashini nods his agreement.

Sinna continues, "Make it between two groups of passengers, not just two guys. Tell him they have been throwing bottles at each other. He may resist, but I'll remind him how important it is for the plan that we get all the way to where he—we—want to go. He'll already be in that frame of mind because of what we'll have been just discussing. A fight in the cabin could put that at risk, especially if people are throwing things at each other that could break windows."

"And when he comes in here I'll restrain him," says Beckman.

"Yes, and I'll turn the aircraft around," Sinna replies.

They all look at each other for reassurance.

"I guess it's the best we can do," Beckman says finally. "Can I be sure he'll come out the same side you did?"

"Yes, he'd be very unlikely to cross over to the other side. But if you sit in 1F, middle of the first row, you can get to him no matter which side he comes out. Aren't the middle seats in row one empty, Faisal?"

"Yes."

"OK, that's what we'll do then. Fifteen minutes, please Faisal," she says and turns for the flight deck.

"Yes Ma'am." Bashini has caught the military bug.

"Good luck, Ma'am," says Beckman.

"You too, guys."

At the door to the flight deck she punches in her access code.

11. THE WAR

"RealWar." I was holding my breath.

"You arrogant son-of-a-bitch." He looked at me like he hated what I had just said, but I saw through the sham.

"Not me. You're the one who wanted to hide in plain sight." He had taken the hook, but I wanted him to swallow the line and sinker as well before I reeled him in, and that was best done by making it his idea.

We were discussing the branding of the new version of TheWar. We'd decided to make it so distinct from the existing games that it needed a name of its own, and the whiteboard was already full of names.

"Very aggressive."

"We are looking for aggressive people."

He was mulling it over for a time, trying it on for size by saying it out loud, writing it down, reading it back, making faces as he went as if to take on different personalities.

"OK Nige, let's go with RealWar. It'll appeal to the kind of players we want."

*

The reaction from players was enthusiastic, and if we had made it commercial, we could have made millions. Instead we recruited millions of hearts and minds. In all sorts of different ways and directions, but all with a common desire to make the world a better place.

Traditionally, terrorism recruited among the angry and the insecure and channeled those feelings into violence, the more the better, but often mindless. What we were planning to do was to recruit among those who wanted to change the world for the better and to do that with as little violence as possible, even if—in what was fast becoming Omar's favourite expression—you can't make an omelette without breaking eggs.

First and foremost it had to have direction. It had to have a mind that people could sense and connect with. And then follow.

All our games had a villain, of course. A dragon to be slain, an evil king to be defeated, a tyrannical emperor to be conquered, but gradually more and more content came closer to reality. The two world wars, the cold war and even recent wars in the Middle East all provided frameworks and context for games, as did wars on drugs barons and even the War on Terror. It was less important to us what the players chose to fight than to gradually make them fight the way we wanted them to fight.

Once the right mindset was cultivated, it was one small step from barons to bankers or from tyrants to tycoons. Especially with people who already bore deep grudges—all we needed to do was give them a little push.

We were taken aback when our profiling showed an enormous level of resentment festering among people in our own business. I suppose it shouldn't have been a surprise. I mean, if we believed these things ourselves then why shouldn't lots of others with similar backgrounds who worked with the same things and got to see a lot of the same muck behind the pretty façades? Corporations who lied and cheated wherever they could, individuals whose private lives belied squeaky clean public personas and not least backstabbing politicians only interested in where the next vote, or the next expenses payment, came from. Not to mention police and others who are paid to look after us but, as we see time and time again, spend much of their time looking after themselves. The whole rotten edifice of modern Western culture.

Most clients choose to ignore, or prefer to forget, that IT professionals get to see a lot of the data behind the pretty pictures we help them to paint. Most handle it the way bank tellers handle money. It's not theirs, they just get paid to count it, organise it and pass it on, but information leaves a stain on people's minds that is more difficult to wash off than the dirt banknotes leave on their hands.

Over time all those fragments of knowledge had stored up a resentment in many of our colleagues, aimed at callous, selfish and immoral people and the ruthless dominance of the masses by a small elite that grows ever richer and more powerful. Not to mention the racist, misogynistic and homophobic occupants of the corridors of power.

Now we were able to tap into that wealth, like prospectors hitting the mother lode, and soon we had developers, administrators and managers in key IT positions ready to do their bit.

At our bidding.

*

Slightly less intelligent were, as it turned out, the intelligence agencies. In their declared war on terror they did all the obvious things. And admittedly all the fun things. Being given the world's largest computers to play with is fun. Being paid to break into public and private network systems is fun. Listening in to people's most intimate thoughts can be hilarious. And it undoubtedly helped catch some bad guys, so it all looked good.

The thing was, it only caught those bad guys who behaved like bad guys. More to the point, who behaved like the spooks' agreed version of bad guys. The main targets were email and social networks, and the harder people worked at becoming invisible, the more resources the snoops poured into looking at them.

It was ever decreasing circles with ever diminishing returns, but as long as all the baddies wore black, it seemed to work. That's why we chose to wear bright red and completely wrong-foot the lot of them. We were so in-their-face subversive that nobody took us for more than we clearly were. A game.

A game so clever that we were even getting increasing numbers of players with IP addresses belonging to the security services.

So our recruits were largely well educated and well placed people who could not be further from the stereotypical picture of a terrorist. Which makes sense, because that's not what they were. We were turning these people into warriors who were going to change the world in ways nobody before had done, and with minimum collateral damage.

We did something else that terrorists stuck in the past mostly got wrong. Instead of excluding half the human race, or relegating them to menial tasks, we actively sought to recruit women warriors. Even though our analyses showed us that, broadly speaking, women are less violent creatures than men, they also showed us how to tap into one of the fiercest forces on the planet: the maternal instinct. Convince a woman that her young are under threat and her fight is more determined, more single-minded and more ruthless than that of any man.

*

"We'd risk a lot more attention from the snoops. They're really focusing on social media now, so I'm not sure it's worth the risk."

We were discussing add-ons to TheWar, and I had aired the idea of a discussion forum or even some kind of network with much more user generated content.

"But I've been thinking about a search engine," Omar added.

"A search engine? Isn't that a huge project."

"Well no, not a metasearch engine. One that interrogates all the other search engines and presents the results as its own. If we had that, we could, ahem, enhance the results to support… whatever argument we want to support."

"We'll have Google on our back." I liked the idea but not the risk.

"Not if we're smart about it. And we're going to be very smart. There's no way anyone will be able to trace where we get our data from. And in any case, we'll produce much of the data ourselves, that's the whole point. Besides, it's just a game, remember? So who cares where we get what in the real world, or if it's accurate. The point is to make players forget where the game ends and reality starts so in the end they believe anything we tell them even if they think they don't."

"Yes, I've got the drift," I said. "Let's not do anything that raises our profile. And especially nothing that makes anyone take us seriously."

"Don't worry, they won't. We're getting a good grip on this subliminal stuff."

If you make someone kick someone else in the head often enough in a computer game, eventually they end up kicking someone in the head in real life. Maybe not literally, but their reactions to violence are gradually numbed because violence becomes the norm. Some people, especially the gaming industry and makers of violent films, argue that, on the contrary, it is a way to act out violence so it doesn't spill over into real life, but evidence suggests otherwise. More and more real violence mimics fantasy violence, not the other way round.

We tapped into that effect to prepare selected players for specific tasks. Not that we planned to kick anyone in the head, but we wanted to use aviation as the key to bringing down Western capitalism. Both because it was such an effective weapon and because seeing that play out on the world stage would be a powerful incentive to the people involved in the next phase. There's nothing better to breed success than success.

That's why we had spent a lot of time looking at airport security and how to get past it. In most places, pilots pass through the same screening processes as everyone else, even if they often have their own channels and are spared the worst of the waiting and the indignities, but security was still an obstacle we had to overcome or bypass.

In the end, it was the way the games developed that gave us the solution. We didn't have to worry about getting anything past security because our pilots wouldn't be carrying anything security could find. They would carry everything they needed between their ears, and no scanner was yet designed that could reach in there.

*

At first, Captain Agung Gupta couldn't see the point of the new games introduced to TheWar. Dubbed RealWar, they promised new levels of sophistication and sense of reality and achievement, but they also required players to give away real information about themselves. All in the name of this new level of reality, of course, but Gupta was wary of it. Was is really necessary, and was there a hidden agenda?

Then he slowly realised that the new games were resonating deeply with feelings he had half forgotten. Memories from his youth in Indonesia; the echoes of the violent struggle between the authoritarian President Sukarno with his communist alliances and his successor, the no less authoritarian pro-American General Suharto. It had left many of his generation with a vague feeling of something lost, something vanquished, and therefore more precious than it was at the time.

Gupta's boyhood fascination with flying developed as he grew older and filled all his time, both as a teenager and as a young man, so he had had little time for politics. Yet the many violent conflicts during Suharto's reign had left him with a sense that things would have been better with Sukarno and the communists in charge.

The focus of the blame became Western capitalism and America in particular. Even though—or maybe because—his pilot training often brought him in close contact with America and Americans, he retained a core of resentment. Who the hell did these upstarts think they were, telling the rest of the world what to

119

do and say and not least think? He felt he came from a culture much older and vastly superior to the West, even if he had to admit the Americans, and by extension much of the rest of the West, were better at making things work.

But it was a world built on sand; it had no roots. That was the feeling he got every time he went to the US on one course or another as part of his pilot training. For all their big talk, Americans were desperate to define themselves as something else. Irish Americans, Italian Americans, African Americans, as if "American" in itself was just an empty shell that had to be filled with something else to have any value. So why were these nonentities running the world?

The new games, RealWar, played on those feelings and satisfied, even if only in the imagination, a desire to try to make things better. On that background it seemed to matter less if he registered his real details as part of the game. It wasn't like they wanted his bank details, just information about his job, his training, his qualifications and a few other things. Things that were no secret anyway, in fact he would have been proud to tell most of them to anyone, so where was the harm?

As it turned out, RealWar soon started earning him a lot more dMons than the old games, and he was able to pay back his virtual loans quicker than planned. Not only was he earning more, but some of the opportunities and choices he was given in the new games also reduced the interest he was paying on the loans. All that didn't matter in the real world, but it was still a relief when Gupta one day paid the last instalment on the dMon loan he had taken out to complete his virtual training and he could start thinking about what else to do with his winnings.

It was around that time he got a new co-pilot and after a while began to play with her. Eventually in more senses than one, but to begin with they were just playing TheWar game. Like Gupta himself, Nurul Sinna had not thought RealWar worth revealing real information for, but under her captain's influence she began to see things differently.

Nurul was too young to share Agung's utopian dreams of a better world under a Communist system but readily agreed that Western capitalism wielded far too big a stick in the world. That was more based on a feeling that there was little difference between the old colonialism and the new globalism. It was largely the same nations that benefitted and the same peoples that supplied the resources and did the work as was the case a century or two ago. OK, they got slightly better paid for it now, and were slightly less pissed on, but the big picture hadn't changed much. Rich man, poor man; rich country, poor country —and for the most part they were the same as always, save for a few oil-rich Arab states who had the West by the balls, and good luck to them. She did not often brood, but when she got to think about these things, a real anger welled up deep within her.

So the direction she took with RealWar was not much different from Agung's. What she did not know was that he had told the Warlords things about their affair that she thought belonged to the sanctity, such as it was, of the bedroom. Nor did it cross her mind that other, former, lovers had told RealWar similar things about her. She would never have told the game such things, but by giving her real name and other details, the Warlords could easily gather all the information on her she thought she was holding back. To such an extent that they now held enough dirt on her to have her over a barrel any time they wanted.

12. THE FLIGHT DECK

Alone on the flight deck, Gupta studies the route ahead on his navigation display. It's just a single magenta line ending in a white star labelled TER THOLEN, but to him it is mesmerising. He is becoming more and more aware of how close he is to making history. He doesn't care about it from a personal point of view. He is not doing what he is doing to get his name into the history books, but to change the course of history for the greater good of humanity.

That's a big stand for one man to take, and the last few weeks he's been on RealWar every spare minute to prepare himself for this mission. The game's own search engine, Dredger, is often much better than Google at finding the things he is looking for. Especially details of his own country's past and the methods the government used to get into power and are still using to stay there.

Much of that goes for every other country that has allied itself with the US in the last half century; in fact ever since the Second World War. They all have a veneer of democracy, but underneath that the reality is that everything is being run by powerful economic forces in the interest of a small elite.

The biggest issues and the most basic needs of the people are callously ignored by this system because they do not translate into easy profits. It would cost ten billion dollars to give everyone on the planet clean water, and about double that to eradicate starvation. Drops in the ocean compared to global military budgets more than fifty times that every year, or the hundreds of billions poured into space exploration with little of true significance to show for itself. But those budgets are paid to the military-industrial complexes of the world. A third of it in one country alone, the US.

What he sees everywhere he looks is the rich getting richer and the poor getting poorer, and that has been spreading even more quickly since globalisation. He is aware that his own job in aviation is a powerful part of globalisation, and that's what has convinced him it makes sense to use aviation as a weapon against it, and to take an active part. He'll be one of a small group of people who are going to fight fire with fire until things change. Whatever the consequences to themselves.

The consequences to the ones he loves are harder to live with. He can't reconcile those thoughts and pushes them out of his mind. He has to if he wants to stay sane and stick to his course.

Suddenly he realises how long his co-pilot has been gone. Must be more than ten minutes, more like fifteen. It shouldn't have taken that long. She might have been delayed by a cabin crew member, but if there was anything seriously amiss, she would at least have alerted him on the interphone.

Or would she? A chill runs down his spine as he understands that she may have turned on him after all and could right now be persuading cabin crew to help her launch some kind of counterattack. Someone could enter the flight deck behind her when she returns and try to overpower him. Once that door opens, he is exposed to attack and the whole project is in jeopardy.

He reaches down to the console and hesitates briefly before he switches the cockpit door lock selector from AUTO to DENY.

That disables the keypad outside the flight deck door and locks himself in.

He has no idea of the consequences. Maybe the cabin will find out what's going on sooner than otherwise, but he knows he is now safe behind a door built to resist terrorist attacks. Everything else on an aircraft is made from plastic or aluminium to be as light as possible, but since 9/11 cockpit doors have been constructed to withstand sustained, violent attack. There is nothing on board that can break down that door or its steel frame.

Should anyone attempt to get through, he'll have plenty of ways to fight back. A few violent manoeuvres would be enough to stop anyone working to break down the door. It doesn't take much to hurt people who are not strapped in, and he has a whole armoury of aerobatics he can use to effectively turn the aircraft into a huge truncheon and batter any attacker to incapacity, oblivion or death.

He can also depressurise the cabin, and at 36000 feet anyone who does not wear an oxygen mask would lose consciousness within seconds, and their life in minutes. Many people think that's a horrible way to die, but it isn't. A brief period of euphoria quickly followed by unconsciousness, then a painless death.

There are portable oxygen bottles for cabin crew, but they can't use those and mount any serious attack on him at the same time.

Captain Gupta, now a full-blown warrior, checks his own four-point harness and oxygen mask to make sure he will be able to carry on fighting no matter what happens.

13. THE CABIN

Bashini and Beckman are still in the gallery, discussing how to deal with a cabin full of passengers who will soon realise that they are flying in the wrong direction.

"Do we bullshit them or do we tell them the truth?" Beckman wonders out loud.

"Most of the time we bullshit them if that's what you want to call it," Bashini answers a little irritably. He doesn't like the big Australian's manner but realises they need the kind of specialist help he offers. "'Cause most of the time it doesn't matter. It's just little things that get cleared up or have no real impact. Delays, things that go bump or whirr. Sometimes we do it because the truth would just make people even more worried and maybe start a panic. Most of them wouldn't understand the real explanation anyway because it's too technical. To tell you the truth, sometimes we don't understand it ourselves but just hope the pilots do."

"Yes but this is not going to go away."

"The worst of it will as soon as Sinna turns around."

"OK, so what do you want to say to them?"

"How about we have taken a more easterly route out over the ocean to avoid violent thunderstorms over the Chinese seaboard and are now waiting for the weather to clear before approaching? That'll explain the changes of direction and the water below if anyone gets to see it. So far it's solid cloud."

Beckman looks speculative. "Hmm. What about later? We'll have to assume we'll be flying north again soon, but we'll be landing in Jakarta, not Beijing. Anyone with the slightest idea of geography will see through that one."

"Yes, but let's worry about Jakarta later. I'd like to tell them only what they need to know to explain what they can see here and now."

"Still going to blame the weather later on?"

"Yes, why not? That is what's screwing up flying most of the time anyway. People expect that."

"I guess."

"And not many people have a real good sense of direction. OK, they know the sun rises in the east and should be out to the right when we're on course to Beijing, but that's about it. Once we start moving around a bit, and the sun gets a little higher in the sky, it's not easy to judge the direction from inside the cabin."

"You're probably right. So if anyone asks you'll say we are flying holding patterns or something like that while we are waiting for weather to clear?"

"Something like that."

"How many people have we got on board?"

"221 passengers and 12 crew, including the two pilots."

"And how many free seats?"

"19 in business and 42 in tourist. Why?"

I'm just thinking if we need to move people around. Isolate someone if they get troublesome before they can spread panic."

"The empty seats in the back are spread fairly evenly. Have to be for weight and balance, so we can't really isolate anyone in them without moving lots of others around. It's easier up front,

128

but the best will probably be row five; it's empty. The five business class seats just behind this galley, before tourist class. They have curtains behind them and the galley in front. We try to keep them empty if business is not full. Makes cabin service easier because they're split from the rest of business in front of the galley. And, to be honest, it gives us a decent place to rest if we get a chance."

"Brilliant. Let's hope we don't need more than that. If we do we'll have to rearrange more business class seats. So if anyone gets too inquisitive you'll get them to move up front. Tell them you'll check with the pilots and could they please follow you. Then we'll deal with it away from the others."

"But we'll have to tell the cabin crew."

"Yes, better get them up here now. Split them into two groups so it doesn't look odd."

"Right away."

*

Sinna punches in her code again. As before, nothing happens. A third time. Nothing. She feels a cold shiver running down her spine as she returns to the galley.

"Faisal!"

Bashini bumps into her just as he is leaving to get his colleagues in the back. "Yes, what's up?"

"My code won't open the door. Can you try yours?"

The two men look at her suspiciously, the creepy feeling returning that there is something she is not telling them. Is she the real problem after all, not the captain?

But then there's the fact that they are still flying south, and the captain hasn't alerted the cabin crew. Logic tells them it must be him, not her, even if their gut feeling tells them otherwise.

Bashini enters the narrow corridor leading to the flight deck and taps in his access code. Nothing happens. Again. Nothing. Then the emergency code. Nothing.

With a sinking feeling, Sinna realises what has happened. "He's disabled the door lock. We can't get in there."

"How can he do that?" asks Beckman who is close behind.

"It's different on different aircraft," Sinna answers. "On this one we have a door lock selector on the flight deck that we can set to Open, Automatic or Deny. Deny means the lock is disabled." She had been so eager to get away from her colleague she had forgotten that he could use her absence to isolate himself.

"Shit!" Beckman nearly hits the door with his big fist, but he knows it will take a lot more than that to get through.

"This has gone far enough now. I want to speak to the captain," Bashini breaks in. "I want his side of this story. Nurul, I know what you say sounds reasonable on the face of it. But with what's clearly an unresolved dispute between the pilots, I have a duty to find out what's what and not just believe one of you. Sorry, but I'll have to call the flight deck."

"Go ahead," Sinna sighs. She realises that she has no choice. It will confirm Gupta in his suspicion, but the damage is already done.

Bashini lifts the interphone handset off its cradle and presses the button for the flight deck.

14. THE WAR

"I think we've got a pair that's ready for the next step. The two in Indonesia who are flying for the same airline." Omar had been sifting through the latest analyses all morning.

"Based on what?" I asked.

"Three things. The way they play, the things they use Dredger to search for and the way they respond to challenges. Especially the guy called Gupta. He's really worked up politically. The woman, Sinna, is very similar, and she's a piece of work. We've got loads of dirt on her. Apparently she's been whoring her way through her whole career. We can ruin her life if we have to."

"So what do you want to do?"

"Keep doing what we have been doing all the time. Confirm and build on their obsessions, tickle their vanity, play on their fears. Only much more so. Start making them numb to really extreme risks. And ultimately accept the idea of dying for what they believe in."

"We could tweak KamikazeHell and add even stronger graphics." I was talking about our most violent aviation game that only accepted players who had gone through the desensitising effects of a series of increasingly blood-curdling games but which still had the power to make them throw up in front of their computer screens. Now I was planning to make it even more vicious.

"Perfect, you go to work on that. It's got to support multi-screen setups; this guy has got one. Never mind 3D for now; he hasn't got the bandwidth." Omar was forever optimising the bang our players got for their buck. And the results we got in return.

"And add subliminal messaging?" I was talking about hidden images and messages embedded in the graphics. It used to be done crudely with single frames of words or pictures cut into movies that showed so briefly they were not visible, but the brain still picked them up subconsciously. It was so effective in advertising that it was banned. With computer graphics we could now do it a lot more effectively. We could tailor-make messages to press the buttons of individual players and optimise them by measuring reactions and refine the message in response. It was made-to-measure hypnotism, highly targeted and phenomenally powerful.

"Absolutely! Pour it on, mostly about America running the world, but also lost childhood nostalgia and how much better it would all have been with the commies in charge. You'll find it all in his profile. Oh, and make him earn a lot of dMons. He's the most money-grabbing commie-lover I've ever come across."

"What about her?"

"Well, as I said, she's a bit of a whore. We know that from what some of the other players tell us, those she has met and used on her way up. It's not direct evidence, but it's pretty conclusive. She's acting the innocent, which I think tells us she's afraid what would happen if it got out. So we should make her absolutely terrified. Apart from that, her main gripes are with globalisation and cultural imperialism. None of his nostalgia stuff, or communist utopia. Not old enough for that, I guess. And she's on a laptop mostly, so we need graphics that kick ass on a small screen as well."

"I'll get on to it."

*

Our plan was starting to come together in ways we had only dared dream of, and we started working seriously on the details of how to make an airliner disappear without trace. Most of the input came from the pilots themselves when we looked at what they did when they played the games. Dodging radar by flying low, tailgating other planes to blend in with them on radar, switching off equipment to confuse controllers and systems, and playing one controller against another in border regions were just a few of the assortment of dirty tricks they came up with.

We were listening carefully and took note of all their bright ideas, so while we were grooming them, they were teaching us. Computer programmers and other nerds call that a positive feedback loop, and we knew exactly how to put it to good use.

What sets flying apart from almost anything else is that pilots are in complete control of everything that happens to an airplane and everyone on it. That's because there is no-one else up there to make the decisions if things don't go one hundred percent to plan, as a lot of the time it doesn't. Maybe there are problems with weather, maybe technical issues, maybe passenger trouble. Whatever it is, nobody on the ground knows about it or has the means to deal with it.

That gives pilots the power of gods. The lives of everyone on board a plane are literally in their hands; much more than on a ship because ships have bigger crews and a better chance that a rogue or mad crew member will be stopped by others. Even so, mad, drunk or incompetent sea captains have caused disasters. In aviation that power is concentrated in only two pairs of hands, and since planes move so much faster, things can go wrong a lot quicker.

These dangers are hardwired into aviation, and all Omar and I had to do was shift the right parts of the equation in our favour. As we got closer to the reality of making airliners disappear, we moved selected players into a flight simulation game complete with real-world data. The plans they came up with could be put into practice any time we wanted, and it was just a question of picking the best among many. Flights could be made to disappear without trace, or they could be crashed in circumstances that pointed the finger at everybody else, inflaming existing tensions or conflicts and making level-headed investigation impossible. The details were not important, as long as the outcome was to make people so afraid of flying that they stopped doing it.

Of course, we were working against everything pilots had been trained to do, but people can be retrained. Reprogrammed. Terrorists aren't born, they are bred. Most of them start out in life as normal, peace-loving human beings, but something turns them to hatred and fanaticism. Radical political or religious views, injustices, tragedies and loyalties are some of the powerful emotions that can push people over the edge, the way we had been pushed ourselves.

This had all been happening for centuries. Our way of doing it was just the latest in a long line, and by far the most effective. Pilots turned out to be as susceptible to our hi-tech brainwashing as anyone else, and we designed different games to train other people to do what was needed in their line of work.

15. THE FLIGHT DECK

Gupta is watching the interphone handset and wonders what to do. The chime has just gone off with a call from the cabin.

It could be Sinna trying to get back in. There could be a perfectly innocent explanation for her long absence, and she might be genuinely surprised that he has locked her out. Whoever is calling, he hasn't had much time since he locked the flight deck door to plan his next move, so he'll have to think on his feet. He will first and foremost have to play it safe.

"Captain speaking," he says in a neutral tone.

"Captain, this is Chief Purser Bashini."

"Yes Faisal, what can I do?" Gupta notices the formality of Bashini's voice and uses his first name to get on the right side of him.

"First Officer Sinna is out here in the cabin telling us that you have taken over the aircraft and you're going to fly it to the southern Indian Ocean and crash it. Please tell me it's not true, Captain."

"Of course it's not true, Faisal. It's the other way round. First officer Sinna tried to take control of the flight and kill everyone by flying off course. I managed to get her off the flight deck, and now I have locked her out. You'll have to deal with her."

"But, Captain, why didn't you ring back and tell us that? Or use the emergency announcement."

"I've been busy working out a new route. Sinna got us so far away from our scheduled route without me noticing that it's

135

difficult to get back to anywhere we can land with the fuel we have left." Gupta hopes to bullshit his way out of his predicament but is none too sure. "I want you to restrain First Officer Sinna and put her where she can't talk to anyone, is that clear?"

"Yes Captain. But I'm not sure who to believe. Sinna's story makes sense. We can see it starting to get light out to port, but if we were on the way north it should have been to starboard as usual. Where are we Captain?"

"She flew us south instead of north." Gupta knows he is on thin ice.

"But how could she do that without you noticing?"

"I was asleep. I'm sorry, it's my fault. I'm working out where we can get back to, but it's not looking good. You'll have to leave me to do my work. Take care of Sinna before she does any more damage." He puts on his gruffest voice to put the purser in his place.

"Asleep? All that time? Captain, I'm sorry but you are making less sense than the first officer. Some passengers are already asking questions. We'll have a panic on our hands if I don't give them a sensible explanation soon." The Chief Purser's voice is increasing in pitch as he speaks.

"Chief Purser Bashini, I have ordered you to restrain First Officer Sinna for attempted air piracy and isolate her from the passengers. Then leave me alone to try to save this flight if I can. Am I making myself clear?"

"No Captain, you're not. This is the first officer's word against yours and hers makes more sense. If you had called us as soon as she left the flight deck, I would have believed you, of course I would. But that was nearly half an hour ago. It doesn't make sense that since then you haven't had time for a single call back to us. It just doesn't. And we're still flying south. If Sinna flew south and you are trying to get back and land somewhere, then why haven't you turned round yet? Captain, you need to open the door and let me in. Please. I'll make sure Sinna is kept away from the flight deck until we clear this up."

Gupta realises he isn't going to pull the wool over the eyes of this senior cabin crew member and simply puts the handset back in its cradle.

16. THE CABIN

"He hung up on me." Bashini leans against the bulkhead and stares at the handset in disbelief, then slowly replaces it.

"What did he say?" asks Beckman.

"He said that the first officer is the terrorist and that he is trying to save the flight from what she has done."

"Just the opposite of what she says, so that's his word against hers."

"Yes, but he is still flying south, and he hung up when I asked him about that. And he couldn't explain why he hadn't alerted us when Sinna left the flight deck."

"What was that about being asleep?"

"He said he was asleep while Sinna flew off course."

Sinna hides a sigh of relief. That's it. Now they have got to believe her. It's lie against lie, but she thinks her lies sound by far the best, maybe because they contain a measure of truth.

"*Asleep!*" Beckman turns to look at Sinna. "*Asleep?*"

"I don't know what to say," she says. "You can hear how ridiculous it is, can't you?"

"All right, that does it. How do we stop him?" Beckman makes up his mind that even if the first officer is dodgy, the real menace here is the captain.

"If we try to break down the door, won't he do what you said he would?" asks Bashini and looks at Sinna. "Do aerobatics and knock everyone unconscious, at least if they are not strapped in?"

"He might. He might decide to do it in any case, just to make sure nobody tries to stop him. We have to get the passengers safely strapped in."

"And tell them what?" asks Beckman.

"That we need them to strap in for turbulence ahead on the route?" suggests Bashini.

"I see. Bullshit," replies Beckman.

Sinna, who did not overhear the earlier discussion between Beckman and Bashini, looks at him puzzled. "No, I think we have to tell them the truth. Or at least as much of it as they need to know."

"Then we need to brief the cabin crew first," interjects Bashini.

"OK, so what about this version of events?" asks Beckman. "The captain has flown the plane off course in a terrorist attack and has now locked the first officer out of the cockpit. We are working on taking back control so the first officer can fly us to safety, and in the meantime we need everyone to strap in securely in case... in case of what exactly?"

"In case of abrupt manoeuvring that may cause injury if unrestrained," sighs Bashini. "Posh words and half baked sentences. Emperor's New Clothes; works every time." He looks apologetic and grimly reflects that his comments might have been funny in other circumstances.

"OK, I can see we can safely leave the bullshitting to you." Beckman nods approvingly at the Chief Purser who starts down the aisle towards the back of the aircraft.

"And Ma'am, I want you to strap into one of those crew seats and stay there whatever happens." Beckman motions to the seats by the forward entry doors, in the curtained-off section between the front of business class and the flight deck. "We can't risk having you hurt if he goes berserk."

Sinna considers his request, but hesitates because it sounds more like an order. Is the power balance beginning to shift? She knows he is right; if she breaks her neck, or anything else vital, they are all done for. But she doesn't like him taking command. She has to be the one who is seen to save this flight.

Beckman senses her reluctance, if not not all the reasons behind it, and decides to soften his approach.

"Ma'am, you're the senior officer here. I'm not trying to change that. I'm trying to protect you. I'm doing the job I was trained for, believe you me." His tone is insistent, but kind, and he keeps the pitch of his voice low, the way he was taught, in order to calm people around him. He could easily have shouted her into submission, but he thinks this will work better.

Right now he is no longer the jaded businessman Ariel Beckman but Staff Sergeant Beckman, SASR, and he hasn't felt this alive in years.

Sinna knows he is right and feels a sudden pang. Beneath her charm, the path she has chosen for herself has made her deeply cynical in many ways, but she realises that this good man is trying to take care of her, the way her father would have tried to take care of her. Not because he wants her but simply because that's what he does. Or at least used to do, but it's still in his blood.

Oh hell, he probably just wants to survive, and who can blame him? She shrugs and unfolds a crew seat, donning the four point harness.

"You're right. Thanks."

Bashini gathers six cabin attendants in the centre galley and briefs them as agreed with Sinna and Beckman.

"But where are we exactly?"

"How could he fly off course if the first officer was there?"

"Why doesn't he crash here and now if that's what he wants to do?"

"How are you going to take control?"

The questions come flying at him faster than he can field them. He holds up his hands.

"I haven't got answers for all that. I only know what the first officer told us. There hasn't been much time to discuss this, and there isn't much time to do anything about it. Our job now is to get the passengers strapped in and kept calm. Anyone who is causing trouble we'll have to isolate up front so we don't get a cabin-wide panic on our hands."

"You'll have to move the whole cabin up front," grumbles one.

"That'll play hell with weight and balance," quips another.

"Enough of that! We have a responsibility to safeguard the passengers as much as we possibly can. You have your instructions, go do your jobs as the professionals I know you are. And send the rest back here for their briefing. Don't say anything to the passengers until I make the announcement." There is a pause in which nobody moves a muscle. "Go, go, go!" he finishes and shoos them away.

In seat 30H, Wong Li Xia is resting uneasily. Her granddaughter, Yan, is soundly asleep under a blanket across the two seats to her left, as are her daughter and son-in-law in the seats on the far side of their centre row. She had watched William twisting and turning for a long time, trying to find rest for his long legs. He first watched the screen in front of him for a while but seemed bored or unhappy with what he found there and finally stuck his legs into the aisle, angled his body awkwardly across the seat and put his head on his wife's shoulder.

It isn't until he takes Ling's hand in his that he seems to find rest. When Li Xia sees that, her last doubts melt away. For all his American manners, she now sees with her own eyes that his love for her daughter runs deep. Men rarely show their true feelings more clearly than just before they fall asleep and become little boys again.

She feels a peace wash over her like she has never known before. She has not known love in her own marriage, but now she knows her daughter does. For the old woman, that's enough for two lifetimes.

But she still can't sleep, and the sudden rushing around in the cabin doesn't help. It's still dark, maybe because the window shades are down, but it may be around the time they are going to wake people for breakfast before landing.

She hasn't flown enough to know much about it, but her senses, and her housewife instincts, tell her it's not breakfast that is keeping cabin crew busy. More like something out of the ordinary. Something that seems to worry them. They rush off to the front of the plane and come back to congregate in the galley in front of her and speak rapidly in muted voices.

The peaceful feeling is seeping out of her again as she starts wondering if it's all too good to last.

*

Up front in his lavish business class seat, which has reclined virtually into a bed, Hamizan enjoys cuddling up to his wife under the blankets. He feels himself getting aroused but quickly moves away a little. He doesn't want to embarrass Ari. Still, this is heaven. Newly-wed, travelling in the style to which he wants them both to become accustomed, and waking up to the smells of fresh coffee and croissants at 36000 feet. Life is good.

From his place by the window—Farah chose the aisle seat because sitting so close to the cabin wall and the emptiness beyond made her uncomfortable—he can see across the cabin to plenty of movement around the curtain that he assumes leads off to the cockpit. A pretty woman in a pilot's uniform dashes back and forth to the galley behind him, and others follow her forward. In his half-sleep he wonders if she is the captain or the co-pilot. The idea of a pretty woman captain appeals to him as he reaches out and gently touches his wife's breast.

But as he comes awake he realises that the activity he is watching is not the normal preparations for arrival. Everything is not as it should be, and he starts sensing something in the air more powerful than the morning aromas. When he sees that the passenger from the seat in front is also involved, he jerks fully awake.

"Ari. Wake up honey," he whispers in his wife's ear, not wanting to wake others or alert the crew.

She stirs and twists round to face him.

"Morning my big man," she murmurs as she stretches. With eyes closed and still half asleep, she forgets where she is.

"Shh my sweet. We're not where you think we are."

Farah jerks her eyes wide open and blushes deeply. "Sorry Hami, I was dreaming," she whispers.

"It's OK, don't worry darling. Listen, please don't be scared, but I think there may be something wrong. I've seen a pilot and a steward and the passenger in front of us, the big man, rush up and down the aisle on the other side and up to the cockpit. I'm just keeping an eye on it for now, but I'll go and check it out if they continue. I want you to stay here if I do."

"Of course Hami. What do you think it is?"

"I don't know. Maybe someone is ill. That's probably it, somebody has had a heart attack or something." Hamizan is growing more and more certain something is not right, but he wants to make it something that is not threatening himself and Farah.

"What are they going to do?"

"Use a defibrillator I guess, or land somewhere to get help." But he sees no signs of emergency equipment or of anyone being treated for anything. It's more like they are worried about something going on at the front of the plane.

In the cockpit. The thought makes him go cold all over.

*

The cabin lighting comes on abruptly and is waking people all around the cabin. Li Xia reaches across the two seats with the sleeping Yan and strokes her daughter's cheek.

145

"Hi mom. Hey, it's light. Did you get any sleep?" Ling opens her eyes and looks at her mother.

"I don't think it's light outside yet, but they switched on the lights in here. I'm not sure, but I think there's something wrong. I think you should wake Jie."

"Wrong? What should be wrong?" She is not fully awake and can't follow her mother's thinking.

"Please wake Jie. The crew have been rushing around for a while without really doing anything, but they're upset about something. I think they are about to tell us, that's why they are waking us up."

"It's just for breakfast, mom!" Ling says.

"No, it's something else. They started preparing for breakfast, then stopped again and started running up and down and talking to each other. I've not been sleeping. I've been watching them all the time."

Ling turns to her sleeping husband. "Jiei, honey, wake up. Breakfast time!" She can't make herself repeat what her mother just told her.

The tall Chinese American slowly unfolds his body and limbs from their uncomfortable position and looks around him.

"Hey, morning. Are we already there?"

"First there's breakfast."

"Oh good. I need the bathroom." He gets up, but a cabin attendant is at his side immediately.

"So sorry Sir. We need everyone in their seats now. There will be a passenger announcement very soon."

"Anything wrong?" William asks.

"The Chief Purser will make an announcement soon, but in the meantime please strap in safely. Is the little girl strapped in?"

"Yes. Can we leave her to sleep?"

"Yes, that's best."

William looks around him and sees that most passengers are awake now and are sitting in their seats with expressions ranging from puzzled to annoyed to angry. Some look frightened. Cabin attendants are waking the remaining sleepers and are calming a few who are starting to ask questions out loud.

A pleasant two-toned chime introduces the purser's announcement.

"Ladies and Gentlemen, this is your Chief Purser Faisal Bashini speaking. I have an important safety announcement. Please listen carefully and follow my instructions. If there is anything in my announcement that is not clear, please contact the crew member nearest to you who will assist you.

"We have a serious situation on board. The first officer has had a mental breakdown and has flown the aircraft off course. The captain is working at regaining control of the aircraft and returning us all to safety.

"In the meantime it is essential for your well-being that everyone remains in their seats and straps in securely in the event of any unexpected manoeuvres which may cause injury if you are not restrained."

*

"What the hell are you playing at," hisses Sinna at Bashini as soon as he hangs up the handset. "*I* have flown off course and *the captain* is working to take control?"

"Sorry Ma'am. I said that to make it all sound a little less bad. I think it's easier for passengers to believe that a captain can take control from a first officer than the other way round. And less worrying that a first officer goes off the rails. We should have discussed it, but it came to me just as I made the announcement. No disrespect intended."

"Good thinking Bashini," Beckman cuts in before Sinna can reply. "And I guess it's not entirely untrue either. With the captain having effectively mutinied, I suppose you're the captain now, Ma'am."

Sinna doesn't feel like a captain, strapped as she is to her collapsible crew seat, taking orders from a passenger and being undercut by her purser.

"All right, if it works. But if you only thought of it right now, what did you tell the crew?"

"Shit, I told them the other way round. I'll get Chanda up here and explain. She's the Senior Air Hostess."

"You do that. And Beckman, you need to get me onto that flight deck." Sinna knows she has to make an effort to fill the role she has been given.

"As soon as the cabin is secure, I'll do my best, Ma'am. What have we got in the way of tools?"

"The only fire axe on board is on the flight deck for obvious reasons. The heaviest things we have are the fire extinguishers and the galley trolleys."

"What do you know about that door?"

"That it's pretty solid and they call it bomb proof, but I'm sure that's just hype."

"Does it have just the one lock?"

"As far as I know, yes. It's not like a safe with pins all the way round, if that's what you mean. Not sure what it'll take to break it, to be honest."

"OK, where do I find the largest fire extinguisher? I'll try to use that as a battering ram."

"What if he starts doing aerobatics?"

"I think I'll be OK inside that narrow corridor. I can brace myself against the walls and ceiling. Worst thing is that whatever I use as a ram might hit me. But I'll have to risk it. It would be useful to have someone to replace me should anything happen. You don't have a rugby team on board by any chance?"

"Hardly, but check with Bashini when he gets back. There must be some other big blokes among the passengers."

"There's no other way to disable him?"

"None that I can think of. The whole system is based on protecting the pilots from the passengers, not the other way round."

"He's a fucking one-man Trojan Horse, that's what he is. Why is he doing it?"

"It's a long story. Mainly because he's angry at America, I think. Or the entire Western world. And he thinks he can help change things by stopping people flying."

"Stopping people flying?"

"By scaring them. An airliner that disappears is pretty scary." Sinna doesn't want to reveal how much she knows; it would implicate her too deeply.

"Crazy idea."

"He is crazy."

"But why didn't you stop him earlier? You could have gone to the authorities or your airline."

"With what? My word against his? A junior first officer against a senior captain, who do you think they would have believed? Besides he was blackmailing me. Never mind how, but things that would harm me. And my family."

"But that's no reason to kill a planeload of people."

"No, and I wasn't going to. It would have worked if I hadn't forgotten that he could lock me out. Or rather, I knew he could but it didn't occur to me that he would. He had no reason to. He was all worked up about me leaving and wanted me back pronto."

"But you didn't come back pronto, did you?"

"I would have if people had believed me," she bites back.

"You told us a pretty tall story."

"No taller than yours."

"Point taken."

Bashini looks relieved when he returns. "Sorted. She thought it was a good idea, too. It won't be a problem in the back."

"Bashini, I need the biggest fire extinguisher you have to batter that door with."

"I'll get it for you. We have one in each galley. Do you want them all?"

"Yes. And I could use some help. Or someone to replace me if anything happens. Have you noticed any big, strong guys in the cabin? Rugby or body builder types. And could you check the manifest for any law enforcement officers?"

"People's jobs are not on the manifest. But I'm sure I've seen some passengers like you describe. Do you want me to get them up here?"

"Yes, please. Don't tell them too much, just that the captain requests their assistance. And let me know when the cabin is secure. Crew too."

"Yessir." Bashini hurries away.

Sinna looks down at her uniform sleeve. "That story about the captain is going to come back and bite us. Lots of people know that captains wear four stripes, not three."

"Why don't you take off the jacket?"

"I have three stripes on my shirt, too."

"Then just leave it. Nobody will notice. They'll have plenty other things to worry about."

"What will you do when you get through?"

"I'll break his neck, don't you worry about that."

"On my say-so?"

"No. His own."

*

Bashir comes back with three men with bodies like fitness centre adverts, but their faces are pale and apprehensive and one of them is gnarled like that of an old man. The Purser has two fire extinguishers with him and goes off for more.

"Gentlemen, I have a story to tell you that you won't believe," Beckman starts. "But I need you to believe it and I need your help. This is our captain. She has been locked out of the cockpit by the first officer who has flown the aircraft off course in an attempt to make the aircraft disappear and kill everyone on board. We need to get back in and let the captain take control. Are you with me so far?"

He looks at the three men who nod back.

"Has any of you got military training?"

The gnarled face holds up a hand. "Yessir. I was a Sergeant, 82nd Airborne Paratroopers. Invalided out of Iraq two years ago. Face held together with steel pins, but otherwise fighting fit. M. J. Walker at your service, Sir." He stands to attention and nearly salutes.

The other two shake their heads.

"Sounds good Walker," Beckman answers the sergeant. "I'm Beckman, ex Australian SAS, and I'm assisting the captain. She is in command, I'm in charge of ops. Our objective is to gain access to the cockpit and restrain or incapacitate the second pilot." He can see the American understands what needs to be done.

"The purpose is to let the captain retake control and return the aircraft safely. You two gentlemen," he turns to the other two, "can be useful in replacing the sergeant and me should we be incapacitated. There is a danger the pilot will manoeuvre the plane so violently that we become injured or worse. In that case

I'll just ask you to do your best where we failed. You are strong men. Will you do that?"

The two men nod with stony faces.

"While we get on with trying to break down the door to the cockpit, it's best if you strap into the first row in the cabin for your own safety."

17. THE FLIGHT DECK

The banging on the door starts shortly after. Gupta's heart jumps at the first loud crashes and his instinct is to make a few violent manoeuvres to stop his attackers in their tracks, but then his pilot training kicks in.

When faced with a crisis, the first thing pilots do is—nothing. Well, maybe not absolutely nothing, but they don't immediately spring into frantic action at any sign of trouble as movies would have you believe. What they do instead is assess the situation as calmly as possible, then take appropriate action. Many more accidents have been caused, or worsened, by doing the wrong thing too quickly than by doing the right thing too slowly.

So he waits, with his hands on the controls ready for a sharp dive which will plaster any intruder across the cockpit ceiling should the door give in, but nothing happens. The banging continues and changes in character from time to time as people on the other side clearly try to break down the door with whatever they can find, but he sees not the smallest sign of any effect. He can hardly see the door shake, even under the most violent blows.

In the meantime he finds time to keep an eye on his dwindling fuel supply. As the distance to Ter Tholen winds down, he periodically recalculates the fuel consumption and makes power adjustments to make sure he runs the tanks dry close to 80 miles from where he wants to crash the aircraft. It is no longer vitally important; they are already so far into the southern Indian Ocean that the wreckage is very unlikely to be found anyway, but he still wants to make it all the way to that deep ocean mountain range and make absolutely sure that the aircraft disappears.

Without trace.

18. THE CABIN

All the seats in business class have been raised to the upright position and Farah and Hamizan are each strapped tightly into their big seat. That means their bodies are suddenly far apart, and the space that felt so luxurious the night before now feels cold and threatening.

"Hami, I'm scared," Farah says in a small voice.

"I know. So am I. But they are doing all they can. I just wish I could do something to help."

"I don't. I want you here. I want to be with you to the end. That's what we said we would do."

"Ari, don't. We'll be all right. These men will make sure it's all right."

Farah starts to cry softly, and Hamizan can hear voices in the cabin that sound like praying. He has no idea what to do other than hold on to his wife's hand for dear life.

*

William Yang feels desperate. He is used to being fairly well in control of most situations, and suddenly his and his family's lives hang by a thread and there's bugger all he can do about it. They have all tightened their seat belts as much as they can, as if that made any difference. He is not sure what they mean by "unexpected manoeuvres" and what could happen, but it sounds like one pilot has gone off his rocker but the other hasn't got control. And what was that about flying off course?

In fact, there's lots in that announcement he doesn't understand, but when it comes to the promised assistance from crew members, they have all gone to their seats and strapped in. One of them is sitting only yards from him by the centre door, and he tries to get her attention.

"Miss, hello Miss!"

She ignores his calls and stares ahead blankly.

She knows no more than we do, he realises, and she is just as scared.

Ling holds her daughter's hand. She is happy the little girl is still asleep under her blanket, safe in her child restraint. Other children in the cabin have started crying as they begin to sense the growing desperation of the adults around them, but Yan is blissfully unaware of it all.

On the far side of the row, the old woman is quietly praying. Not that she believes devoutly, but more because she doesn't know what else to do, and it calms her a bit. She reaches out to her sleeping granddaughter and touches her little body through the blanket.

She had not wanted to come on this journey and had argued with her daughter about it. Then at some point during this night suddenly her entire life made sense and she finally found happiness. Now she is just a little sad that the life of the young will be so short, but she is glad she is with them when the end comes, as she feels sure it will, because she could not have borne losing them.

She knows not why, and she does not really understand all that is happening around her, but she knows they are all going to die very soon.

*

Beckman and Walker, the American, have been hammering on the cockpit door with the heavy fire extinguishers with no visible effect. The door easily absorbs even the heaviest blown they can throw at it. Their armoury is limited, and the space they have to work in confined, but they are still surprised to see not the slightest effect of their prolonged pounding.

They are even more surprised that the captain hasn't made any move to defend his position. He must have great confidence in that door, Beckman thinks. Or know something we don't.

In the meantime, Sinna has remained firmly strapped into her crew seat and kept her head down in her smartphone, tapping away furiously. Typical, Beckman thinks during a pause in the onslaught. Wouldn't be surprised if she takes a selfie next. He's not sure typical of what. Women? The young? Just anyone other than himself.

"There is something else we could try," Sinna says and looks up. "I've been doing weight and balance, and I have an idea."

"Weight and what?" Beckman wipes the sweat off his face and finds it difficult to make the connection between a smartphone and the very real fight for their lives they have on their hands.

"And balance. Calculations pilots do to ensure that the aircraft is within limits of weight, and more importantly balance. The weight has to be distributed evenly or we become nose heavy or tail heavy. In both cases the pilot loses control, but here's the

159

thing. If we make the aircraft tail heavy, it will stall, and that just *may* be survivable."

Beckman looks at her incredulously. "*Stall* the plane on purpose?"

"Yes. I can't be sure, but some of us may survive a relatively slow stall into water. At least the automatic distress beacon would deploy. Even if we die, we won't disappear. People will find us and find out what happened and the kind of terror he is planning will fail. I know it doesn't sound like much, but it's better than what Gupta has in store for us."

"How many people do you need to move?" The Australian knows it's time to hedge his bets, especially with his first bet not looking to come off.

"We could start with moving everyone from business to empty seats in the back."

"That's only a dozen or so."

"Sixteen. No, not enough, but it's a start, and it'll fill 16 of the 45 free seats in the back. Then we need to move another 29 in tourist back in the remaining empty seats. And put all cabin crew in the aft galley. That's 230 people—everybody except you, me and Gupta—all in row 15 and back. That'll put us more or less on the aft limit, but we need to make people in rows 15 to 17 or 18 move further back to make her stall."

"Her?"

"Sorry. The aircraft." Sinna is one of those female pilots who actually like aircraft, and ships, being referred to in the feminine. It endows them with an air of life which serves as a reminder to treat them with the care and respect they need. She always does so herself, and she secretly pats every aircraft she enters and leaves, like a treasured horse. She therefore forgets that many outside the business find it archaic or demeaning.

"Ma'am, with all due respect, that's the most insane idea I've ever heard."

"No, it isn't. Crashing an airliner with 233 people into the ocean at a location never to be discovered is more insane, and I thought you had realised that's what's going to happen if we don't stop it," Sinna shoots back furiously.

Beckman bites his lip. "Yes Ma'am. I see what you mean," he says quietly.

"Another thing. We should tell passengers to shoot as many pictures and videos as possible, and leave voice recordings on their mobile devices. The more there is of that kind of thing, the better the chance some of it will be found," Sinna continues.

"But they only have the half-baked story about the first officer flying off course. That'll put the blame on you. And if we ask them to leave messages for their loved ones, they'll panic. It's the same as telling them they are going to die."

Sinna knows that. "Can't be helped now. But you're right, we mustn't panic them. Never mind, they'll do it without being told. Do you think you can get them to move?"

"Shouldn't we try the door one last time?"

"No point any more."

"What?"

"It's a quarter past six, Singapore time. We are now past the point where we could have made it back to land anywhere."

"You're sure about that?"

"Yes. Flight planning. It's simple maths, I do it every day. It's my job."

"But there are reserves."

"That includes the reserves. Every drop of fuel on board. Don't forget that's how the whole thing was planned in the first place. Down to the last drop."

The legs give way under the big Australian. He has exhausted himself physically and mentally, believing it would give them a fighting chance. It has now all come to nothing, and he slides onto the floor and hides his face in his hands.

"Sir, I'll assist you if you'll allow me." Walker has been through worse than this. He actually died in Iraq when the explosion hit him in the face, before they revived him and patched him back together as best they could. He has lived with searing pain ever since, and a second death holds no fear for him.

Beckman looks up at the old face of the young American. "No need to call me Sir. I was a sergeant like you. Let's go do it."

*

"Ladies and gentlemen, can I please have your attention." Beckman stands at the front of the business class cabin and speaks in a clear and firm voice.

"We need to move you briefly to the rear of the aircraft for your own protection." He points to the cabin attendants they have assembled at the back of the cabin. "Please follow cabin staff who will show you where to sit. This is a temporary measure and you will return as soon as it is safe to do so."

Bullshitter, he screams inwardly at himself as he watches people get up and walk to the back of the cabin, the young couple holding hands as they disappear through the curtains. He is sick to the stomach with disgust at what he is watching himself do because it seems such an extension of what he has been doing for far too many years. Lying, deceiving and double crossing, all in the name of somebody else's game.

When they start moving people in tourist class further back, a stocky man in his forties stands up in the middle cabin and starts shouting at him.

"What's this all for? Our protection! How stupid do you think we are? If you move everyone to the back of the plane, we'll crash. Ladies and gentlemen, please don't move anywhere until we have been told what is really going on. We are being lied to and treated like cattle. It's got to stop. We are *people*, not sand bags."

Beckman realises a shouting match is not going to lead anywhere and tries to reason with the man.

"Sir, if you'd like to come with me, I'll be glad to answer all your questions."

But the man stands his ground. He is in the middle of row 20 with other passengers on all sides, so can't easily be isolated. Maybe that's what gave him the courage to oppose Beckman, or maybe he is just that kind of man.

"If you can answer all my questions, then answer this. And I don't need to move anywhere for you to do that. You can answer in front of all of us. What exactly is it you are protecting us from by moving us back, and what is happening to the plane's weight distribution if you do? Like I said, the people here are not idiots."

"Sir, you don't understand. The captain has calculated the aircraft's weight and balance very carefully and it is safe for you to move back. But you are right, we are trying to force the pilot who is now in control to change course, and we are trying to do that with the onboard weight distribution."

"That's crap!" shouts the man. "Are you a pilot?"

"No, I'm not."

"I'm a glider pilot. This man is lying to you, folks, and he knows it. We want to see the captain and have him explain what is going on."

"Ladies and gentlemen, please, for your own sakes," tries Beckman. "Move to the rear of the cabin. This man may know about gliders but not about airliners."

"Why won't the captain speak to us?" asks one.

"Just get the captain," shouts another.

"We don't believe you. Who are you anyway," yells a third.

"The captain is busy getting back control of the flight…"

"See, that doesn't make sense either," shouts the stocky man. "*Busy getting back*, what does that mean? Either he has control or he hasn't. What's this shit about getting back? Back where? Hey, has the other pilot locked him out of the cockpit? Is that it? In that case he can't get back in, isn't that the whole point about protecting the cockpit? Is that what all the banging has been about? In fact, come to think of it, who's to say *you* are not the terrorist? Looks much more like it to me than anything else."

The mood in the cabin is turning ugly, and Beckman knows he is losing whatever tenuous grip he might have on things. Now is the time to extricate himself before it turns physical.

"OK, OK. I'll try and get the captain for you."

He knows he can't. This man will immediately spot Sinna's three stripes and the whole situation will unravel. Just the fact that she's a woman could tip the cabin into revolt. Dammit, just one little slip made for what seemed like good reason.

Anyway, he never really believed this idea was going to wash. One thing is having your life threatened by a terrorist, committing mass suicide is quite another, and people know the difference when it stares them in the face.

*

From his front seat in the rear cabin, William has been following the shouting in the centre cabin. The passengers that were, more or less, frogmarched to fill the empty seats in the rear made no sense to him, but now he thinks he is beginning to understand what's going on. There seems to be a fight over control of the plane, and passengers are being used as dead weight to bring about some effect or other.

He looks across at his family and thinks about what they would want him to do. His mother-in-law looks like she is praying, while holding on tightly with one hand to little Yan who is still fast asleep. Ling is just staring blankly at nothing in particular.

He takes her hand but can't find anything to say that makes any sense. He wants to ask her what to do, but is afraid she will tell him there is nothing he *can* do.

*

Farah and Hamizan are crammed into the two seats in the far left corner of the cabin, but at least they are closer together than in their big seats up front. In fact, sitting at the very back gives them an odd feeling of, if not control, then some kind of perspective. They have a view of the entire rear cabin and can see past the galley into the middle cabin. Up front their posh seats kept them apart even from the few other passengers in their cabin, but now they can see the hundreds of fellow travellers. Or at least the tops of their heads.

Subdued sounds of praying and crying mingle in the cabin, but most people are quiet. Many are tapping away at their electronic devices, leaving messages of love and pictures of waving hands and faces with forced smiles.

Loud discussions are still going on in the middle cabin, so when the change in engine sound comes, few passengers notice. It just goes a little bit quieter. To the young couple in the very back it briefly feels like someone pushes their seats to one side, then the other, almost as if the plane is wagging its tail.

But everyone hears when the second engine stops. It is as if all sound stops, as if the whole world stops. Then a sharp descent starts, much steeper than a normal descent, and people's ears begin to pop as the cabin pressure starts dropping. With no engines to keep the cabin pressurised, the air slowly escapes through natural leaks.

The cabin lights go off and the dim emergency lighting comes on, plunging the cabin, still with most blinds lowered, into a gloomy darkness even as the dawn lights up the eastern horizon.

Batam flight 8125 is on approach to its final destination.

19. THE WAR

As we got closer to a launch date, it turned out that Sinna was not as easy to win over completely as her colleague had been, so in the end we fed him the information we believed would keep her in line. We knew enough sordid details about the way she had built her career not only to ruin her but scandalise her entire family. She didn't have any children, but we hoped her defensive instincts would kick in to protect her elderly parents who would be left completely disgraced if their daughter's behaviour came to light. That sort of thing mattered in small villages in Malaysia.

But it was too much of a risk to carry on like that, so we decided not to have two pilot warriors working together in future. It was also difficult to get two warriors into the same cockpit, the way airlines worked their rosters. The Gupta and Sinna couple had dropped into our laps by chance. The pair of lovers were already engineering their rosters to be with each other as much as possible, but we didn't have any other matched pairs in place anywhere. We'd have to find a way for a single pilot to carry out an attack.

"Can't one pilot lock the other one out?" I was thinking out loud.

"Yes, but that relies on the other pilot wanting to leave the cockpit at the right time, and that's not something we can be sure of. We also don't know exactly how strong those cockpit doors are. Maybe they can be broken down. Or passengers may be able to raise the alarm with mobile phones or something, depending of where they are. Too many unknowns."

"Need to knock the other pilot out, then."

"Yes, and you know what. A handful of the sleeping pills I take would knock out a horse." More than four years after his attack, Omar was still regularly using strong sleeping medicine.

"Hmmm. But how do we get someone to take sleeping pills without knowing?"

"We put them into something they don't suspect. There's just five milligrams of active ingredient in each of my pills, the rest is filler. We could extract the, the benzo… whatsitsname, and make it into something that could be dropped into a drink."

"Worth a try. But that would depend on our warrior pilot being able to get the same sleeping pills. And follow our prescription exactly."

"Or we could just send them the extract when we work out how to make it. Much simpler, and then we know they get something that works."

That was a small risk worth taking.

*

It wasn't as easy as it sounded, but we got there with some trial and error. The toughest thing was for Omar to get by on over-the-counter sleeping aids while we used his prescriptions for our concoctions. We crushed his tablets and dissolved them in water, then filtered them through a coffee filter. The first time it all got sucked into the filter and nothing came out the other side, so we learned to wet the filter first to allow the solution to drip through. The fluid we made was bitter at first, so we tried to add different things to mask the taste. When we tried maple syrup, we ended up with a fairly bland liquid that was tasteless when squirted into a cup of coffee or a soft drink.

We then worked out a dose that was sure to put a person into a deep sleep quite quickly but not too quickly, because the victim had to have enough time to drink up. A few millilitres of the stuff was enough, but we still had to get it past security without raising questions. Our solution was to put it into the innocuous little eye moisturiser bottles that many frequent fliers carry because of the dry air on airliners. They were small enough to pass through the ban on liquids without problems, and we even worked out a way to keep the original seal on the bottles intact.

We had invented a weapon nobody else had thought of, so nobody was looking for it.

20. THE FLIGHT DECK

Captain Gupta doesn't notice the automatic trim system gradually winding on more and more forward trim as passengers move to the back of the cabin, but when the right hand engine runs out of fuel and spools down, he watches the autothrottle push up the power on the left hand engine to try to maintain the selected speed as the autopilot feeds in rudder to compensate for the asymmetric thrust. The loss of half the power of the big airliner is therefore fairly uneventful, no more than a gentle wag of its tail, and Gupta calmly reaches out to cancel the alarms that go off as he watches one of the two sets of engine instruments drift down to zero.

But both engines are fed from the same central fuel tank, which is in turn fed from tanks in the wings, now long empty, so it takes less than a minute before the second engine fails. This time the effect is more pronounced. The loss of engine sound is plain to hear, and the autopilot pushes the nose down to maintain the selected airspeed. The final descent has started, precisely 80 nautical miles from Ter Tholen. Gupta is happy with his navigational craftsmanship.

He wonders briefly what is happening back in the cabin since the banging on the door stopped. But he is more focused on making sure the last phase of the flight goes to plan. They are descending at the speed he set for the cruise, Mach 0.80, but as they get into denser air he'll have to reduce that in order not to exceed the aircraft's maximum speed and risk damaging the wing or tail. If that happens at altitude, the aircraft would create a large debris field, and he wants one that is as small as possible.

There's also the ram air turbine to consider. With no fuel on board, both engines and the auxiliary power unit and their generators are out of action. He has electrical power for the instruments and autopilot from the batteries, but the power he needs for the fly-by-wire flight controls comes from the air turbine which automatically drops out of the belly of the aircraft and into the airstream if the generators are lost. There is a maximum airspeed at which the turbine can operate, and if he exceeds that he will damage it and lose all control of the aircraft.

On top of all that, he has never flown a glider before in his life. After hours of inactivity, Captain Gupta suddenly becomes a very busy man in the final minutes of flight AB8125. He works as carefully as he ever did. It's partly the routine of a lifetime of flying, but more importantly he simply sticks to the plan he has for this particular flight. That will make it easier to go through with the final few seconds, he hopes.

As the aircraft descends towards the ocean, the grey dawn in the east glows brighter and shines on a solid cloud cover below. Gupta hasn't got the barometric pressure at this position to set on his altimeter, so he doesn't know his exact altitude, but at around fifteen thousand feet he enters the wet, grey mass. Ice immediately starts building on the windshields because the electric deicing doesn't work without engine power. He knows he will be getting lashings of ice on his wings too, but with the speed he is keeping that shouldn't be a problem.

At six thousand feet the ice starts to melt again and flies off the windshield in big chunks. Gupta switches off the autopilot. He is going to hand fly the last few thousand feet because he needs to steepen his descent beyond the capability of the autopilot in order to build up speed. He wants to hit the water at almost the speed of sound for maximum destruction. That increase in speed may start to break up the aircraft before it hits, but he is now so close to the end that it doesn't matter.

At three thousand feet he breaks out of the overcast, and the sight of a menacing, blue-black ocean that abruptly fills the windshield hits him like an iron fist. Whitecaps from mountainous, breaking waves flicker wildly before him, and the last conscious thing Gupta does in his life is to push his flight controls fully forward into a vertical dive for the highest possible speed at impact.

The end comes first to the flight deck, but only by a few hundredths of a second.

The airliner hits the water at a speed of nearly a thousand feet per second, about 90% of the speed of sound. It is 200 feet long which means that the tail arrives at the same place one fifth of a second later, or in the blink of an eye.

For the aircraft to slide into the water as gracefully as a highboard diver into an Olympic swimming pool, it would have to displace its own entire volume—around five hundred thousand gallons—in that fifth of a second.

Since it cannot do that, there is nothing graceful about the end of Batam 8125. What happens is exactly what would have happened if it had hit a mountain.

21. THE CABIN

When the nose is flattened against the water, which is hard as granite due to the velocity of the impact, a shock wave starts moving back through the aluminium body of the airliner at the speed of sound. Sound moves in aluminium more than six times faster than in air, so the shock wave moves through the entire length of the aircraft in about thirty milliseconds.

The aircraft moves in the opposite direction at a slightly more leisurely one thousand feet per second and therefore takes two hundred milliseconds to crash into the water. As a result the shock wave reaches everyone on board before they actually crash, and that is one small blessing.

After three milliseconds, the shock wave reaches First Officer Nurul Sinna who is still strapped into her crew seat in the forward galley area close behind the flight deck door. It travels through the seat into her buttocks and up through her body as what would appear on a high speed camera as just a small bulge in her skin. When that bulge hits her head with the power of a steam hammer, her brain instantly ceases to exist as a collection of interconnected, living cells holding all the consciousness, memories, hopes, dreams and life of a human being and is transformed into the mindless mass of an indeterminate biochemical paste.

Seventeen milliseconds later, the same happens to the family in row 30. The little girl is still asleep in her seat as the shock wave races through her and her father, her mother and her grandmother, and they all cease to exist.

The last to die, at twenty-five milliseconds from impact, are the young honeymooners in the two seats at the farthest corner of the rear cabin. The shock wave rips through their hands as they sit close together in a tight grip only microseconds before it reaches their brains. At that instant, all Farah's shining bubbles burst and drift away.

Not a single person experiences even the briefest moment of pain, or awareness of their fate, before the terrible, physical destruction arrives.

No-one except Ariel Beckman who is in the centre galley trying to fashion a heavier battering ram from one of the galley trolleys. He knows the flight is doomed, but he still wants to get into the cockpit and at least get a message out to the world. Because he is not strapped in, he floats in mid-air in the few seconds of the final plunge. So the shockwave doesn't touch him, and the last thing he sees and hears, for a split second, is the terrible crushing of everything in front of him before he is smashed to pieces himself.

Since the water cannot move out of the way as fast as the airliner moves forward, almost half a million pounds of metal, plastic, glass and human beings are compressed and torn into billions of fragments from smaller than a pinhead to no bigger than a fingernail in the space of a fifth of a second.

Half a dozen or so solid chunks of aircraft structure, such as engines and landing gears, survive in large pieces, even though mangled as if run through the hot rollers of a steel mill. They immediately start their vertical descent to the ragged mountains more than a mile below the surface.

Everything else mixes with water into a pulpy mash that slowly spreads and begins to sink. All marine life for hundreds of feet around the impact zone is killed by the shock wave spreading through the water, but slowly nature's processes blend back into the cloudy remains of an airliner with 233 souls on board and start the relentless business of absorbing, dissolving and eating them.

Before long, the perpetual motion of giant waves rubs out the tiny stain on the vast ocean, and the last traces of Air Batam flight 8125 and all on board her finally disappear from the surface of the Earth.

Never to be found.

22. REAL WAR

AIRLINER DISAPPEARS WITHOUT TRACE

HOW CAN 233 PEOPLE VANISH IN MID-AIR?

FLIGHT FROM SINGAPORE TO BEIJING MISSING

SUSPECTED TERRORISM IN AIRLINER DISAPPEARANCE

Air Batam flight 8125 from Singapore to Beijing has disappeared, and the story is top of every TV news channel and on the front page of every newspaper. All sorts of people are falling over each other to advance one theory or another: it was shot down, it has flown to Iran, it is on a Pacific island, it was Israel what did it! The coverage is even more frantic, and much of it more fanciful, than we had hoped, and Omar is beside himself with excitement.

"See, I told you. It's working. It's the biggest friggin' flying story since Lindbergh crossed the Atlantic. And it's going to get bigger when they don't find anything. Nothing!"

"I know, Ome. I just wish I was as happy as you are. But we've killed 233 people."

"That's not the way I look at it. More than six thousand people die *every hour* all over the world, for all sorts of reasons. One hundred and fifty thousand a day! Of which more than three thousand are traffic accidents. Stupid, unnecessary *traffic accidents*, for crying out loud! Another 233 makes no difference in the scheme of things. Except, actually, these people *will* make a difference. Their deaths will come to *mean* something. *We* have made sure of that."

"All right Ome, I know all that. I just can't jump for joy."

"NEITHER CAN I!" He screams it at me and would have hit me if he could have got out of his wheelchair.

"Omar, I know what they have done to you, and I know how you feel. And I have started, so I'll finish, because if I don't then it *will* have been meaningless. But what we are doing is not making me happy. I'm sorry, but that's the way it is," I say and leave the room. I can't face him just now.

In fact, as news stories go, this is probably no bigger a story than when Air France 447 disappeared over the South Atlantic five years ago with 228 people on board. But then some wreckage was found after a few days and people learned what had happened, and where. The story died down after that, even if it took two years before anyone knew the reasons why it happened.

But this time they won't find anything, and that will keep the mystery alive and make them have to go on looking. They will spend tens if not hundreds of millions, and they will start fighting about who is in charge, about how to interpret every piece of evidence they think they find, about where to look next, and finally about the costs. Especially about the costs.

In the meantime I have no other choice but to go on preparing one pilot after another to continue the fight.

23. THE FLIGHT DECK

Captain Paul King settles into his left hand seat and starts on the stacks of paperwork that these days seem to be the most important pieces in the giant jigsaw needed to get a transatlantic airliner off the ground and headed westward.

The puzzle is so vast now that it has to be delegated out to a large number of people. Planners, dispatchers, loaders, engineers, meteorologists; people he has to trust have done their job properly by the time he hurls five hundred tons of airliner down the runway and into the sky. He hasn't the time, or even expertise any more, to do it all himself.

When he was a young pilot, flying was much more hands on, literally. He got to see and touch many of the vital parts of his aircraft every day. And even if the flight plans were filed by the pretty girls in the operations office of the small airline he worked for, he checked each plan in detail and marked it on his charts before flight, making sure that an update or a restriction hadn't been overlooked. Then he checked actual and forecast weather at his departure point, destination, alternate and all along the route. He worked out the fuel he needed and supervised the fuelling. He personally took samples of the fuel from the tanks afterwards and smelled it, even tasted it sometimes if anything seemed out of the ordinary.

Like when a fuel filler cap had been left off overnight and gallons of rain water had run into one tank. It looked, and even smelled, like aviation fuel because it came from the tank and had taken on its smells, but there was something about the way it moved in the jar he collected it in that was different. He dipped a finger in it and licked it. Pure water. That could have snuffed out an engine, maybe on takeoff.

Today his P2, or first officer, Jason Rana is doing the walkaround, such as it is. More of a ritual than a real check, if only because anything of significance is out of reach on today's big jets. It feels more like a case of "kick the tyres, light the fires," as pilots used to call an inadequate preflight check.

Captain King knows it's safe enough, because the army of people he relies on are all doing their jobs, but he still feels a little uncomfortable about it. A little out of the loop. On the other hand, he is glad not to be out in the wind and rain on days like today.

"All OK, Capt'n," the fresh-faced first officer breezily calls out as he steps onto the flight deck and hands over the fuel manifest he just collected from the fueller on the ground.

"Thanks. Bad night out there?" King says just to make conversation. It's the first time he flies with this young pilot and he wants to put him at ease.

"Yes, and it's getting worse I think." The young man hangs up his wet overcoat and slides into the right-hand seat that's traditionally the first officer's position. He adjusts the big seat to make sure his feet reach the rudder pedals and he can work the flight controls comfortably.

Then the two pilots get on with the routine of getting ready for departure. The captain starts his briefing.

"OK, this flight is from Heathrow to JFK. We expect a Compton Standard Instrument Departure from runway 27 Left via

Woodley. The planned route is Compton, Upper Lima niner to Strumble. Our oceanic entry point is MALOT, then track Echo to five-one north, five-zero west, then ALLRY. The SID and the route are in the flight management system. After the SID, initial flight level is 340, and 400 from three-zero west. Alternate is Newark. Flight time to JFK is seven hours ten and we have fuel for eight forty. I am PF and you are PNF on this leg. Any questions?"

Rana has no questions but studies the Standard Instrument Departure chart to remind himself of the all important climb profile: above 3000 feet at 11 nautical miles after departure, above 4000 feet at the WOD beacon four miles later and 6000 feet eight nautical miles before the CPT beacon. They also have to reduce power at specific points, all in order to cut noise on the ground, and microphones along the flight path are monitoring their departure to make sure they do. Their airline will be fined if they exceed the noise limits, so as pilot-not-flying, one of his jobs is to make sure the pilot-flying adheres to all these demands.

As PNF, Rana also operates the radios to get the latest weather report and clearances, and relays all this to the captain. The flight deck routine flows smoothly, and King is satisfied with his young colleague. He does not generally hold these 1000-hour pilots in high regard, partly because he recalls how ropy he was himself at that stage of his flying, but he has to admit that the training they get these days is probably better than what he got. Regular simulator sessions and serious crew resource management training is a lot more useful than circuit bashing in light aircraft at the local flying club and mean that a second officer's job is no longer "gear up, flaps up, shut up" as it was in his own youth. He is not entirely free from being a little envious.

Then, on the other hand, he wonders how long young pilots have in the job with both airlines and aircraft manufacturers itching to bring in pilotless aircraft. The only thing holding them back is fear of a passenger backlash. A bit like why passengers still face forward in flight when it is well known that rear facing seats are much safer. But people simply won't accept that, so no airline is going to introduce it.

With margins as thin as they are in aviation, flying is now an industry that only survives on volume. The biggest fear of every airline is anything that makes people fly less, because just a little less could start a negative spiral that would make the whole industry collapse. Aviation is poised on a very sharp edge.

*

Just under an hour into the flight, they are settled at flight level 340 and approaching their oceanic entry point, 53 degrees north, 10 degrees west. Rana has obtained clearance to enter the North Atlantic westbound track system from Shanwick Oceanic, and their next reporting point is 20 degrees west, in about 50 minutes. Then 30 degrees west, where Gander Oceanic takes over. All is well.

"OK if I take a break now, capt'n?"

"Sure, go ahead Jason. I'll mind the shop." Captain King is relaxed, and his initial good impression of Jason Rana has only improved. This young man is on the ball. Knows his stuff and keen to get ahead. Does all the right things, asks all the right questions and listens to all the answers.

What King does not know is that Rana's brother was killed in Afghanistan a year ago. He was a soldier, fighting what he believed was a necessary war, because everybody told him it was.

184

His name was Thomas Rana, except he had changed it to Saif al Din, the sword of the faith, when he converted to Islam several years earlier.

Their family hailed from Hindu stock but had lived in Britain for generations and were not really religious. Even so, Thomas joined the Taliban to fight for what he had come to believe in passionately, and he had died horribly in an American drone attack along with 36 others, mostly civilians including many children.

On this night exactly a year ago.

"Anything I can bring back?"

"Yeah thanks, a black coffee. Two sugars, and if you can find some of those chocolate chip cookies. The dark ones."

"Will do, capt'n. Be right back." First Officer Rana had relied on that reply. He had yet to meet a captain who did not want a cup of coffee or tea once the busiest part of the flight was behind them.

*

At 9.40 PM London time, they are passing 20 degrees west, and Rana radios their position report to Shanwick Radio on the shortwave radio as they are now outside VHF radio cover.

"Shanwick Radio, Eureka 840, position."

"Eureka 840, Shanwick Radio, go ahead."

"Eureka 840, passed five-four north two-zero west at two-one four-zero zulu, flight level three-four-zero, mach point eight-two, estimating five-four north three-zero west at two-two three-zero, five-three north four-zero west next. Eureka 840."

The calm, professional routine chatter of one of the nearly fifteen hundred aircraft crisscrossing the North Atlantic every day, although much of it is now done via datalink. Hundreds of miles from land, there is no radar cover out here, so air traffic control relies on pilots reporting their positions at specific points. And on them telling the truth.

Rana is going to keep up the procedure for the next three reporting points, at 30, 40 and 50 degrees west, but when he makes those reports he will be further and further away from where he says he is. With no radar cover, no-one will be the wiser, and then, when his aircraft fails to appear on radar for its North American landfall, it will seem suddenly to have vanished into thin air.

Captain King has been fast asleep since about half an hour after his young, eager co-pilot brought him coffee and chocolate chip cookies. When he started to feel drowsy shortly after, he began to shift in his seat and tried to exercise the muscles in his abdomen, buttocks and legs to improve blood flow and clear his mind. But by then it was too late. The medication Rana had added to the coffee kicked in quickly, and he passed out before he knew what was going on.

Now in sole control of the transatlantic flight, Rana sets in motion the plan he has carefully worked out with the help of the aircraft manual and checklists to ensure that he does not leave an electronic footprint. First he switches off the satellite communications system that provides both data communications and telephone links for the passengers. Then he calls the cabin.

"Green speaking."

Rana recognises the senior cabin attendant's voice. Sophie Green; he has flown with her before and fancies her, but she is one of those annoying, happily married types.

"First Officer Rana here. Just wanted to let you know that we have lost satcom for some reason. We're looking at it, but it could take a while. You might also lose your flight map if we have to reset some systems." He is making it all up, but the cabin crew have no way of knowing that.

"Oh, all right, thanks. Not a big problem, most of them are asleep now."

Rana knows that, it's all part of the plan.

"I'll let you know when there's any change."

He reaches down and switches off the flight map system that lets passengers follow the flight's progress on their screens. He does not bother to mute the cockpit voice recorder. He is not going to talk to himself, and anything he says on the radio will be completely routine and only confuse anyone who listens. Not that anybody ever will.

Then he switches the autopilot to heading mode to keep the aircraft steady before he starts reprogramming the flight management system. He deletes the flight plan to New York and substitutes a single waypoint: 23 degrees north, 45 degrees west.

That's in the middle of the Mid Atlantic Ridge, an underwater mountain range twice the length of the Himalayas. He names the point KANE after the fracture zone at that position, 2200 nautical miles away. The Kane fracture zone is a particularly rough stretch of seabed, well away from shipping lanes. It has been chosen for all those reasons, and because it is the most remote spot in the

North Atlantic with over a thousand nautical miles to land in any direction. That means round trips of two thousand miles for search aircraft, which makes things very difficult if anyone should ever think to look in such an unlikely place.

Jason Rana doesn't know exactly what happened to the missing Air Batam flight. But he knows that he is about to carry out the second disappearance of as many as it takes to bring aviation to its knees, and with that the financial systems of the hated enemy who murdered his brother.

He selects 5 degree banks on the autopilot and switches back to navigation mode. The big airliner leans into an imperceptible left turn and settles on its new course towards the empty Atlantic Ocean.

*

Two and a half hours later, Jason completes his last position report to Gander Radio on shortwave and is handed over to Canadian domestic air traffic control on VHF:

"Eureka 840, passed five-one north five-zero west at zero-zero one-two zulu, flight level four-zero-zero, mach point eight-two, estimating ALLRY at zero-zero two-three. Eureka 840."

"Eureka 840, reaching ALLRY contact Montreal Centre on 133 decimal 22."

Jason answers with the terse, rehearsed reply that will from now on make controllers' blood run cold while they reach for their alarm buttons:

"All right, good night." The signoff from Hell.

Jason is nowhere near the position or the altitude he reports. He has remained at flight level 340 and is a thousand miles to the south-east, passing four hundred miles west of the Azores on a south-westerly heading running parallel to the Mid Atlantic Ridge. Shortwave radio signals have a long range because they bounce off the ionosphere, but that means they are non-directional, so controllers have no way of knowing where his transmissions are coming from.

He then switches off all his radios and starts preparing for the end.

The distance to Kane is almost the same as to New York, and with the fuel he has on board, he will have enough for an hour and a half when he gets there. That's five thousand gallons of jet fuel that he does not want to have on board when he crashes into the ocean because it will leave too much of a fuel slick for someone to find. He could have descended earlier on in order to burn more fuel at a lower level, but a simpler solution on this model of aircraft is to dump fuel. Not all aircraft have the ability to do that, it depends on the difference between their maximum take-off and landing weights, but this one has.

The fuel dump check list tells him that he can pump 1250 pounds of fuel overboard per minute through each wing tip nozzle. That's a total of 300 gallons a minute, so he needs to dump for 17 minutes to lose the excess fuel. From 34000 feet, and over a distance of 140 miles, the fuel will evaporate long before it reaches the ocean and not leave any trace on the surface. He times the dump carefully and keeps an eye on the fuel management system at the same time to make sure he has precisely enough left to run the tanks dry 80 miles before Kane.

*

Jason keeps the cabin crew happy by giving them the usual briefings at the usual times. The flight time to Kane is going to be much the same as to New York, and all the normal cabin activities can be kept up, so no-one will have any reason to suspect anything is amiss until the final few seconds.

"One hour to landing. ATC have advised they are going to keep us high all the way in, so the descent will be later and steeper than usual, better prepare the passengers for that. Let me know if you want me to come and tuck anyone in, such as yourself."

"Thanks Jason, that won't be necessary. Anything we can bring you?" Sophie Green thinks Jason a bit fresh, but she likes the young pilot and doesn't really mind. She just takes it as a compliment to an old, married woman as she jokingly calls herself.

"No thanks, we'll be busy from now on. There's a bit of weather down there as well," he adds to explain the absence of any lights below as they are supposed to approach over the eastern US seaboard.

"Oh, and apologies to the passengers that we couldn't get the satlink back. Some avionics snafu," he adds airily and leaves it to Green to come up with an explanation the passengers will accept.

"Will do."

That should keep the cabin crew busy, but just in case, he turns the flight deck lock to DENY. He doesn't want any visitors now.

*

When the tanks run dry and the engines die, Jason starts his descent into the infinity of the darkness below. It is close to 10 PM Eastern Standard Time, the time they should have landed in New York, but because they have not been flying as far west, the local time is midnight out here over the middle of the North Atlantic. It doesn't get much darker than that anywhere on Earth.

He keeps the speed as high as he dares and descends at three to four thousand feet per minute. When his radar altimeter shows they are 2000 feet from the ocean, he still can't see anything in the blackness outside, but he pushes the nose into a vertical dive to build up even more speed.

Jason's last thoughts as he feels himself become weightless are of Thomas, his identical twin, who was cold-heartedly murdered in an aerial attack on this night a year ago.

Eureka 840 hits the water in complete darkness, and everything ceases to exist in a blink of an eye. Another airliner has been swallowed up by the vastness of the oceans.

Never to be found.

24. REAL WAR

AIR INDUSTRY IN CHAOS

ANOTHER AIRLINER MISSING

TERROR IN THE SKY CONTINUES

FLIGHTS CANCELLED WORLD WIDE

PLANE DISAPPEARS OVER NORTH ATLANTIC

"How many this time?" I ask Omar who is scanning the news.

"286. But more to the point, it's working. Second hit, and people are already taking to the hills."

"Can't we stop it here and get on with some of the other lines of attack? On the IT infrastructure, either of the airlines or the banks or both at the same time. Something that doesn't kill people." I am nauseous with disgust at what I am doing.

"Depends." He eyes me grimly. "If people are scared enough now, then yes. But if they start flying again any time soon, then no. No follow-up, wasn't that what you said about the old terror? If we don't follow this up, then we're making the same mistake and everything we have done so far will have been a total waste. Over five hundred people will have died for nothing."

That's the way he keeps egging me on. If we don't succeed, then those people died in vain. If we do, then they died for a reason. Who am I to take that away from them?

"But we could attack the infrastructure now. That would be the follow-up." I am desperately trying to get away from killing more people. Even when you don't do it with your own hands, it eats away at your soul. If you have one. I am beginning to wonder if Omar does.

"That only works if they're already on their knees. I'm not sure they are yet. People have short memories and the airlines will swing their damn PR machine into action. Buy all the press they can. We need to keep up the pressure to stop that. The media are for sale, and the only thing that will make them tell the truth is if it keeps happening."

"Ome, I can't keep doing this. It's worse than the night they came for you. I thought that would be the worst thing that would happen in my life, but this is much worse. That night we were innocent. The fuzz were the fucking bastards. Now we're the fucking bastards. I just can't keep doing it. Don't clobber me with your statistics. I know that five hundred people die all over the world every five minutes, twenty-four seven. And I remember telling you that as many die every year from ear infections as died on 9/11, but I'm not the one murdering them. These five hundred died because of something I did." Saying the number out loud makes me dizzy.

He rolls his wheelchair up close to me and puts his hand on mine.

"OK Nige, I can see that. What is it you want to do, then?" he says softly.

"As I said, roll out the attacks on the infrastructure. Airlines first. If we hit the booking systems just as people start to want to fly again, if they do, it'll be the knockout that'll send them over the edge. Then we hit the banks. Clearing systems, currency systems, trading systems, it's all lined up and ready to go."

"All right. Let's give it a rest for a while and see what happens. Maybe we can do it your way. I'll keep the kettle on the boil; you take a break."

*

PACIFIC PLANE MISSING

AIRPORTS STAND EMPTY

PANIC GRIPS AIR TRAVEL

L.A. TO TOKYO FLIGHT VANISHES

EUROPEAN AIRWAYS FILES FOR BANKRUPTCY

"YOU FUCKING DOUBLECROSSING MURDERING MANIAC. YOU SCREWED ME. WE HAD AGREED. GIVE IT A REST YOU SAID. SEE WHAT HAPPENS YOU SAID. TAKE A BREAK YOU SAID." I am screaming at the top of my voice, and the only reason I am not going at him hammer and tongs is because he is in a wheelchair.

"I know what I said. I said for you to take a rest, and that I would keep the kettle boiling. This pilot was good and ready, and we needed to throw a third punch. Now three major routes have been hit, and people know it can happen anywhere in the world. Maybe we can give it a rest, we'll see."

"YOU killed 266 people. Not me this time." I end on a whimper.

"I can live with that."

That's when I snap and hit him. I slap him across the face with all the force I possess in my skinny body. Which isn't a lot, but enough to tip his narrow indoor wheelchair over, maybe from his recoil as much as anything. It crashes on its side with him in it, and he knocks the top of his head against a table leg with a grinding sound that I haven't heard since that night. Afterwards he lies deathly still with blood gushing from a deep cut on the head and one arm at an awkward angle under the wheelchair.

I stand transfixed and stare at the devastation I have just wreaked. Omar's blood is collecting in a pool under his face and he is not moving a muscle. I can't even see him breathe. It dawns on me that this time I may have killed a human being with my bare hands. In an argument which was more about betrayal than about people, or even about conscience. More about me than the five hundred people I had killed. We had killed.

That's when it hits home. We. Not I. This is about something we have done together, and it is something we must finish together. I can't change horses midstream. I knew from the start people would die, and accepted Omar's argument that fewer people would die if we did this than if we did not. The time to argue had been then, not now.

The trance lifts and the first thing I do is check his pulse. I can't find any. I leave him on his side; better with the head low, I think. He may bleed less if he sits up, but I'm not sure I can get him up and not hurt him more than I already have.

I dial 999 in a panic, speculating like mad if it's now 112 or 911 or something else entirely. Why do they fuck around with things like that?

"Emergency services, what do you require?"

"Ambulance, please. My partner has tipped his wheelchair and hit his head. He is unconscious and bleeding."

Suddenly I realise that bleeding is good. Bleeding means that the heart is pumping blood round his body, even if I can't feel it. Bleeding means life.

I start crying hysterically and have difficulty giving them a coherent address.

*

"You Brits are getting too violent for me. I want to go home to America," is the first thing Omar says when he wakes from surgery.

Another broken arm, a concussion and ten stitches to the top of his head. They have shaved the crown of his head which makes him look like a turkey. An angry turkey, but sarcasm is oozing from his every pore as he speaks.

Sarcasm is good, I think with a sense of relief. If bleeding means life, maybe sarcasm means forgiveness. If he had been angry and cold and quiet, I would have been afraid, but now I think we may be all right.

"Sorry Ome," is all I can get out. I reach for his hand.

He takes it. "Don't be an idiot. Just a lover's tiff." I can see he means it. "But let's not tell anyone that. I tipped because I was trying to lift the dinner tray from the side instead of in front as they've taught me. A stupid weight and balance error."

I've hit him, could have killed him, and all he is thinking of is that I don't get into trouble over it.

"OK, if that's what you want to say. I've just said you tipped, which you did, but not why. But that fits."

"I want to go home as soon as I can."

My heart is in my mouth. Home to America? Is that what he wants anyway?

198

He sees the fear in my face. "No, not that," he says quietly. "Home to us. You got to convince them you can look after me. Don't want to stay here a minute longer than I have to."

He's had enough of hospitals for a lifetime.

*

I can't convince them. They probably suspect what happened. Hospital staff have a sixth sense about injuries—not that that helped us when Omar had his back broken by the law. But the black eye he got when I hit him doesn't really fit the rest of the story. We invent a tall tale about the tray hitting him in the face when he tipped, but they still insist they can't let him go before the swelling goes down. There's a danger of pressure on the brain, and there could be secondary bleeding.

So when he gets back after a week without computer access, the world has moved on at warp speed. The social media are ablaze with theories of all kinds, dozens of books and films are on the way, and everybody and his grandmother is airing their opinion in the media. Which is everything we hoped for, because it adds nothing useful but just pours petrol on the fire and spreads the panic.

"The airlines say they have made sure it can't happen again. Only problem is that they still haven't explained how it happened in the first place, so people don't believe they know what they are talking about."

"Does anyone even listen to them any more?" I ask.

"Not really. Sorry to rub it in, but it was when the third one disappeared that their PR people lost all credibility. You can keep a lid on it once, maybe twice, but not three times. Have you been following what's happening financially?"

"Trading in airline shares has been suspended almost everywhere. Governments are mooting guarantees, but the banks are still jittery as hell. Smaller airlines, and airports too, have started laying off short-term staff and furloughing contract personnel. The unions are kicking and screaming, and companies are fighting for survival."

Omar isn't looking as happy as I thought he would be. I've got over my scruples and am more worried about Omar staying in the UK. Staying with me. I know I'd never get a US green card.

"But is there talk of banks folding?" he asks.

"Not a word. Not yet anyway."

"Or even any serious problems?"

"Nope, tight as a drum. Which probably just means that they are managing to keep it under wraps for now."

"How much flying has stopped?"

"They say that more than eighty percent of flights are getting cancelled. Those that do go are pretty full. There are still people who stick one finger up at danger, or are more or less forced to go. Besides, those flights are full of air marshals and police and whatnot. There are more guns on airliners now than on fighter planes."

"Bloody hell. Eighty percent cancellations and those that do fly have to cost them a fortune with all that extra security. They must be losing billions." He starts to look a little brighter.

"OK, so here's what I've been thinking," he continues. "We probably can't get at any more airliners just now anyway, so we'll leave that alone. What we should concentrate on is fanning the flames. Especially the fear of what else might happen. Make people afraid of their own shadow in the end."

"Are we talking global or local?"

"Good question. If it's local it should be something that makes people think it could happen in their neighbourhood next. What have we got?"

"We've got people inside oil, power, trains, banks, insurance, shipping, defence, communications…"

"Maybe that's it. Communications. Remind me, what can we do?" Omar interrupts me.

"Pretty much anything, I think. From shutting down a few links short term to sending satellites out of their orbits."

"Whoa, whoa, careful there. We don't want it to break down completely just now. We need the satellites to spread the panic. We want something spectacular without shooting ourselves in the foot. You're the one with the bright ideas," he adds in a teasing voice.

"Currency exchanges. We've got warriors inside the IT systems of the London, New York and Tokyo exchanges. If they crash those systems and shut them all down just for a few days, we'd stop a lot of trade and make everyone jittery as hell. Exactly what we want; make them wonder what happens next."

"Brilliant. Let's do it."

*

DOLLAR DROPS IN CURRENCY TURMOIL

CURRENCY CRISIS HITS INTERNATIONAL TRADE

CURRENCY EXCHANGES ATTACKED—WHAT NEXT?

FREIGHT RATES COLLAPSE ON FEARS OF TRADE STOP

VANISHED PLANES LINKED TO ATTACKS ON EXCHANGES

"Happy now?" Omar asks as he pushes the iPad across the table.

"Yes. Especially the one about freight rates. The Baltic Dry Index is already down eleven points."

"Meaning?"

"Meaning that if it continues, shipping companies will lose even more money than airlines because they'll get paid less for moving goods around than it costs them to do it, and running big ships is even more expensive than running airliners. Then the values of their ships collapse because everybody wants to get rid of excess capacity at the same time. Both of those things will put enormous pressure on banks because both ships and charters are heavily mortgaged."

"I thought shipowners were rolling in it."

"They used to be, back when they operated clapped out old tubs and charter rates were sky high because there weren't enough ships after two world wars so competition was low. Now they've been building ships for sixty years, competition is cut-throat, everything's mortgaged to the hilt and they're operating on paper-thin margins that can vanish overnight for a thousand different reasons. Very much like the airlines."

"You almost make me feel sorry for the bastards."

"What I'm saying is that we can do a lot of damage to the Western economies through shipping." I nearly add "instead of killing people" but bite my tongue. No need to open those wounds again. Water under the bridge, and I have to admit it did get the ball rolling.

Instead I add, "Banks have huge exposure to shipping. More than they had to those subprime mortgages that caused the crash in 2008, and shipping is worse in a sense, because it's on their books as low risk. When the real size of it is exposed, a lot won't survive. And those that fail will bring down others."

"All right, let's get some banking IT warriors lined up to add to the fun when this shit hits the fan."

*

DOMINO EFFECT IN BANKING SECTOR

OIL PRICE COLLAPSES ON LOW DEMAND

BANKING COMPUTER SYSTEMS BREAKDOWN

AVIATION BANKRUPTCIES ADD TO BANKERS' WOES

BANKS UNDER PRESSURE FROM SHIPPING COLLAPSES

GOVERNMENT DECLARES BANK PLEDGE UNAFFORDABLE

"This is snowballing exactly the way we thought it would." Omar punches the air with his fist which looks faintly ridiculous from a man in a wheelchair.

"Yes, and we don't even need to do anything to the oil industry. It's doing it to itself. Prices have halved in the last month because producers can't agree to limit output to demand."

Omar looks nonplussed. "But lower oil prices are good for the economy?"

"They are if lower prices mean that industry can make more stuff at a lower cost. Not when they are low because manufacturing is collapsing."

"And that collapse is adding to the shipping collapse."

"Exactly. You're getting the picture!"

"Are you enjoying it now?" he asks.

"Yes, but it scares me too. It's got a life of its own."

"Welcome to parenthood," he replies mockingly. "We made this baby, you and I. Now all we can do is watch it grow. Which reminds me. We've only used a fraction of our warriors. Many of the rest are getting impatient. They want to be part of this, now they see things happening in the real world."

"Yes, but we've got to keep them on a leash. Can't have this spiral out of control."

"Not sure how much control we have. Or should have. We've created these guys, and gals, let them go and do what they want to do."

"But the idea was to control it from here," I argue.

"Yes, in the beginning. To get it started, and we did. But now it's so big, and so complex, it's getting beyond our control. I think we should give those who're chomping at the bit a free rein."

"That'll be dangerous."

"Revolution is dangerous."

*

ROAD, RAIL TRAFFIC AT STANDSTILL

FOOD RUNNING LOW IN LARGE CITIES

ARMY CALLED IN TO CURB CIVIC UNREST

GOLD AT ALL TIME HIGH IN FRANTIC TRADING

SEWAGE SPREADS DISEASE AFTER PUMPS CUT OUT

GRID COLLAPSE CAUSES NUCLEAR POWER MELTDOWN

The next wave of disruption hits electricity where it is most vulnerable. The electric power grid is vast and looks extremely robust. But although it is everywhere around us, its details are invisible, but far from invincible. The grid is run by a network of controllers, and its soft underbelly is the software they use. Attacking that software and making it fail causes the system to crash spectacularly.

When that happens, separate sections of the grid shut down and isolate themselves for protection. This leads to overproduction in other sections, which in turn leads to more shutdowns. In the end the entire grid falls apart. Oil or gas or coal fired power stations can shut down in response fairly quickly, but nuclear plants have a colossal inertia and take up to a week to shut down. If they are forced off the grid abruptly, they are very difficult to bring to a gentle stop but risk overheating and melting down.

With transport and many large industries shut down, currencies and shares go into free fall. Banks are failing left, right and centre, and governments abandon attempts to bail them out. That makes people flock to put their money into precious metals and gems, and those prices go through the roof, which only adds to the volatile mix.

Bank and computer failures close down credit card systems, and cash machines quickly run out of bank notes. People then start raiding shops just to get necessities, and the looting soon spreads to luxury stores. Entire city blocks burn down as firefighters are attacked by mobs wherever they turn up to protect life and property.

Our war on the West is biting hard and is having real, long-term consequences. Just as we wanted. But it is frightening to watch all the same.

*

NATIONWIDE BLACKOUTS

HOSPITALS TURN AWAY PATIENTS

CHOLERA EPIDEMICS HIT MAJOR CITIES

WARLIKE SCENES IN DENSELY POPULATED AREAS

SATELLITE FAILURES CAUSE COMMUNICATION CHAOS

WORLD TURMOIL TRACED TO ONLINE COMPUTER GAME

"Shit, our cover's blown!" Omar turns pale as he reads the article with details of how satellite operators found out who have been inside their most sensitive systems. It looks like cyber attacks, because that's what it is, but the agents of those attacks come from deep inside their own ranks.

Someone left a door ajar on purpose, but that someone did not cover his tracks well enough. When he is traced, they don't jump on him right away but monitor him and find out what he is doing and who he is talking to.

That's how they find TheWar.

"But that doesn't mean they've found everybody else. Or us?" I ask.

"I don't think so. It looks like they haven't got into our systems, but that could just be a question of time. We need to shut it all down, and fast. Everything is so heavily encrypted we don't have to worry about the data we leave behind on the servers, but we need to stop warriors accessing it so they can't be traced. The question is whether they can trace it back to us if they look long and hard enough. They'll do all they can, that's for sure."

Of course we have been using every dirty trick of the dark net all along, including software such as Tor, so nothing we did at any point could be connected with us. Those things are protecting money launderers, paedophiles and other common criminals as well as legitimate do-gooders like whistleblowers and their contacts. But it's anybody's guess whether it will protect someone who is attacking society on the scale that we are. It has never been done before.

With everything collapsing around them, maybe security forces won't have the resources to look for us as hard as they need to. Or maybe they won't find us before electrical power becomes so scarce they can't run their supercomputers. Only time will tell.

In the meantime, with devastating momentum, the thousands of warriors we have trained and prepared will continue, no matter what happens to us. Then copycats will join them, as we have seen with riots and civil unrest, and the real war will go viral.

AVIATION GLOSSARY

Air Traffic Control (ATC)

Air Traffic Control controls the flow of air traffic within *Controlled Airspace* (CA). Whenever possible this is done with the help of ground based *radar*, and the job of controllers is primarily to keep aircraft separated both vertically and horizontally.

In remote regions such as oceanic crossings, where radar is not available, ATC is "procedural" which means that controllers and pilots follow specific radio communication procedures where pilots report their positions at given intervals and controllers note the progress of flights based on these reports. This is slower and less accurate than radar control, and aircraft separation is therefore greater under procedural control.

While ATC *controls* aircraft, pilots are still in *command* of aircraft. The distinction between command and control becomes important when pilots need to do something other than what the controller wants or expects. This could be a diversion around uncomfortable or dangerous weather (which ATC cannot see on radar), or for some technical reason, or because onboard events (e.g. passenger illness) demand a change to the flight plan.

Airway

Airways are 'highways in the sky' designed to keep aircraft moving in an orderly and predictable way and keep them separated.

Each airway has a name consisting of one or more letters and a number, such as M765, UN866 etc. An airway consists of a number of *waypoints*—at least one at each end, but normally a string of them. Waypoints have names like EGARI, IGAMO, IPRIX, ODONO etc.

The position of every waypoint is known to the navigation computers of modern aircraft, so pilots just have to use the waypoint names when entering their flight plan. This is much quicker and safer than keying in complex latitude and longitude positions as was done in early navigation systems.

Following every twist and turn of airways can add many miles to an aircraft's route, increasing costs. Pilots therefore increasingly ask for 'direct routes' and are often given them when *Air Traffic Control* has the required information (from *radar*), the right equipment (computers) and enough capacity to do so. In such cases aircraft will leave the airways and follow the shortest route from point to point, sometimes hundreds of miles apart, but responsibility for separation still rests with *ATC*.

Alternate

Short for 'alternate destination.' Every flight plan has to designate an airport other than the intended destination in case weather or other circumstances prevent landing there as planned.

Altitudes and Flight Levels

The altitude of an aircraft is measured in feet or metres above a fixed level, called a datum. Two datums are commonly used: a specific runway or the mean sea level.

Altitude is measured by an instrument called an altimeter, and each pilot has one of these in his primary field of vision. The instrument works by simply measuring the air pressure outside the aircraft because air pressure decreases with altitude. So the lower the pressure, the higher the altitude, but in order to indicate the actual height above a given datum, the instrument has to be set to the barometric pressure at that datum.

Therefore, in order for the altimeter to show height above a particular runway (Above Ground Level - AGL), pilots have to set the barometric pressure at that runway. They get this information from the airport, and when so set, their altimeters will show zero when landing.

That system is useful when close to an airport but no good at separating aircraft in the air because the datums of various airports are not the same. Instead, the altitude Above Mean Sea Level (AMSL) is used when aircraft move away from the immediate airport environment.

In order to indicate AMSL, the altimeter is set to the pressure at the mean sea level. This pressure varies across the face of the Earth with the movement of high and low pressure systems associated with weather, and a large number of 'regions' have been created, each with its own 'regional pressure,' which is the average pressure across that region. Altimeters must be reset as aircraft move from region to region in order to show the correct regional altitude AMSL.

The use of local airport pressure is falling into disuse, and most pilots now land with regional standard pressure set. This means that their altimeters do not indicate zero when they land, but the altitude of the runway.

At high altitudes, where separation from the ground is of much less importance than separation between aircraft, a third system is used. This is called 'standard pressure' and means that all aircraft in this airspace set their altimeters to 1013.25 Hectopascal (or Millibar as it used to be), or 29.92 inches of mercury. This means that all aircraft in this airspace measure their altitude to the same, artificial but constant, datum.

To make it clear that this indicated altitude is not an exact height above any ground feature, it is called a Flight Level (FL) and is expressed as indicated altitude divided by 100. Thus 20,000 feet becomes FL200, 35,000 feet becomes FL350 etc.

There is another way of measuring height above the ground or water: the radar altimeter (RadAlt). All large aircraft have RadAlts, but they are only used for low level flying, typically below 2,000 feet, and especially as an aid during landings.

See *Q-codes* for explanations of QFE, QNH and QNE as these terms relate to altimeter settings.

Black box

A common name for an aircraft's *Flight Data Recorder* and *Cockpit Voice Recorder*. In fact, these recorders are painted bright orange to make them highly visible amongst aircraft wreckage.

The name 'black box' is thought to come from various secret electronic equipment installed on many WW2 aircraft, usually in boxes that were actually black. The contents of these black boxes were known only to few, so the term 'black box' came to mean anything that was a bit obscure and not widely known or understood.

A lot of aircraft electronics (avionics) to this day come in boxes that are painted black. In fact most things do—except the so-called 'black boxes.'

Cockpit Voice Recorder (CVR)

The Cockpit Voice recorder records sound from the flight deck of an aircraft and the radio communications between pilots and *ATC*. The sound is obtained from each pilot's headset microphone, from an 'area microphone' in the roof of the cockpit and from the radios pilots use to talk to ATC.

Sound is recorded in a loop, with current regulations requiring 2 hours of sound available at any one time.

Controlled Airspace (CA)

Airspace is divided into a number of areas, both vertically and horizontally, each of which has a particular set of rules associated with it. The most strictly regulated airspace is Controlled Airspace, and most airliners spend most of their time there because it is well regulated, looked after by *ATC* with *radar* and therefore the safest place to be.

It is also an expensive place to be as the cost of ATC with all its personnel and high tech equipment is levied on aircraft flying in controlled airspace. In some places (such as the US) this charge is paid through an aviation fuel duty, in other places (such as Europe) the aircraft operator receives a separate bill for route charges.

Estimated Time of Arrival (ETA)

The time of arrival at a destination that a navigator calculates, based on either the Estimated Time of Departure (ETD) or the

Actual Time of Departure (ATD) plus the Estimated Time En route (ETE).

The Actual Time of Arrival (ATA) consists of Actual Time of Departure (ATD) plus Actual Time En route (ATE).

All these components are used in navigation because things rarely go exactly to plan. Departures get delayed (not often the opposite) and en route times get both shorter and longer depending on winds, re-routings and traffic delays.

Flight Data Recorder (FDR)

The Flight Data Recorder (also known as Accident Data Recorder, ADR) makes digital recordings of a large number of facts surrounding an aircraft, such as heading and altitude, speed, engine settings, control surface positions and movements, fuel state etc. etc.

With this data it is possible to re-create a flight in every detail, normally done mostly for accident or incident analysis.

Data are recorded in a loop, with around 20 hours of data available at any one time.

Fuel

Jet and turboprop airliners use a fuel called Jet-A1, which is similar to diesel except for the contents of various additives and the strict control of water in jet fuel. This is because aviation fuel can cool to considerably below freezing during long flights at high altitude, and significant water content could freeze and cause problems in the fuel system.

Pilots work with three different properties of fuel: volume, weight and endurance. They are related, but not in a simple way.

The fuel *volume* is important because an aircraft's tanks have room for a certain maximum volume. Fuel is also delivered to the aircraft, and charged, by volume. Either litres or gallons depending on location (and even gallons come in two sizes, US and Imperial, but most places using Imperial gallons have now gone metric).

But volume varies with temperature because fuel has a large expansion coefficient. For example, one thousand lbs (454 kg) of Jet-A1 varies in volume from 140 US gallons (530 ltr) at −40°F (-40°C) to 150 US gallons (570 ltr) at 104°F (+40°C).

The fuel *weight* is important for two reasons. Firstly because fuel is a large part of the total weight of an aircraft (up to more than half), and the amount of fuel on board can therefore be restricted by weight as well as volume, depending on the weight of passengers, baggage and freight on board.

The other reason is that it is the fuel *weight* that determines the amount of energy and therefore the *endurance*, and ultimately how far an aircraft can fly on a given amount of fuel. For example, an aircraft that burns 20,000 lbs of fuel per hour will fly six hours on 120,000 lbs of fuel, no matter if that fuel takes up 17,000 or 18,000 gallons of tank volume.

Latitude and Longitude

A system of coordinates that specify the north-south (latitude) and east-west (longitude) position of any given place on the Earth.

Latitude has the Equator as zero and extends to 90° N and S, the position of the geographical poles.

Longitude has the Greenwich meridian as zero and extends to 180° E and W, on the exact opposite side of the Earth.

For example, 54°N, 20°W is 54 degrees north of the Equator and 20 degrees west of Greenwich. Similarly, 33°23′S, 77°45′E is 33 degrees, 23 minutes south of the Equator and 77 degrees, 45 minutes east of Greenwich.

Nautical mile (NM)

A nautical mile is 1.15 statute miles. Nautical miles are used for navigation, both at sea and in the air, for the simple reason that it is a natural component of the system used to indicate position: degrees, minutes and seconds (see *Latitude and Longitude*). Nautical miles can therefore be read directly off maps that are marked with these intervals.

One nautical mile is one minute of arc on a great circle. Since there are 60 minutes to the degree, one degree of arc on a great circle is 60 nautical miles.

The Equator is a great circle, and so are all meridians—the lines on a globe that pass through both poles and denote *Longitude*. The shortest direct distance between any two points on the earth is also a great circle. This is useful for ships and aircraft which try to follow these shortest possible routes as far as practicable.

When speed is measured in nautical miles, it is referred to as 'knots'—not 'knots per hour,' just knots (meaning nautical miles per hour). It refers to actual knots on a line used to measure speed on the sailing ships of old. The speed was indicated by how many knots ran through the fingers of the navigator in a given time when a wooden 'log' with the knotted line attached was thrown into the water. The log was a triangular piece of wood that was kept vertical in the water, and therefore relatively stationary behind the moving ship.

Terms such as 'log' even for a modern ship's speed indicator and 'log book' for the written record of a ship's progress derive from this piece of wood. To this day, pilots also keep detailed log books of both their own flying hours and for each aircraft they fly.

Navigation

Navigation consists of two main elements: The art of knowing exactly where you are at all times and the craft of knowing how to get from where you are to where you want to be without bumping into anything on the way.

Apologies if that sounds flippant, but it sums up navigation, even if it is now less of an art and more of a science after electronic navigation—especially GPS—has taken much of the hokus pokus out of it.

Hundreds of thousands of lives have been lost at sea and in the air over the centuries because navigators did not know with sufficient accuracy where they were. They relied on often fleeting glimpses of the sun, moon or stars to tell them where they were on the surface of the Earth. Even at its best, the accuracy of astro navigation was measured in miles, and at its worst it was little better than the next best thing: dead reckoning.

Dead reckoning means keeping a record of your movements in terms of direction, speed and time and working out your position based on a previously known (or assumed) position, plus these movements. A simple example: if you start out from X and proceed due south for 10 hours at 10 knots, you would think you end up 100 nautical miles south of X.

Well, maybe you do, sort of, but not exactly. Wind and tides will in all likelihood have pushed you one way or the other during those ten hours, so much so that you may be perhaps 50 miles from where you thought you were.

Navigators do their best to compensate for these things, but don't always have all the information they need, so the new position will be uncertain to some extent. You then use that uncertain position as a starting point of the next leg of your dead reckoning, and your circle of uncertainty gets bigger and bigger.

GPS has removed most, if not all, of this inaccuracy and uncertainty, so most of the time we know within feet where we are, and accidents at sea and in the air have dropped dramatically as a result.

But as anyone with a GPS in their car knows, knowing where you are does not necessarily mean you get to where you want to go. It is still a craft to work out the best way to get from A to B. On the roads it involves choosing the roads best suited to your vehicle, ones that are not one way in the wrong direction, taking the right, sorry correct, turns at the correct times and so on and so forth.

At sea and in the air, the shortest possible route is preferred, which is often a direct one. But it can only be used if there are no obstacles in the way, such as shallow water or mountains, airspace or sea lane restrictions, weather, other traffic or a thousand other things. So here's the rub: In order to avoid these obstacles, routes are usually *not* simple point-to-point lines, but a series of complex doglegs that have to be followed with great accuracy.

A lot of the craft that goes into planning and executing these routes is now also performed by electronics, but not without supervision and intervention by humans. Some of the black art now consists of knowing how to operate your GPS and get around its quirks and limitations, and some of the craft on how to cheat it when it tells you to turn down a one way street or into the teeth of a thunderstorm.

So even if navigation is now largely science based, it continues to be part art, part craft. And more than ever, it relies on people other than the navigator. Just think of the army of people who maintain the integrity of the GPS satellites and their signals and the mountains of data, collected by humans or at least with human intervention, that those signals need to relate to the world around us.

Pilot roles

Pilot-flying (PF) and pilot-not-flying (PNF) are the two roles of the pilots on board. The captain, also called pilot-in-command (PIC) or P1, is always in overall command of the flight, but that does not mean that he or she always handles the controls. The pilots normally take turns, so the first officer, or P2, flies half the 'legs,' as one flight from departure to destination is called.

In certain circumstances, such as landing in particularly challenging weather conditions or with technical problems, the captain, as the most experienced pilot, will take the controls, even if the first officer is PF on that leg. However, in many other emergencies, the captain will take on the PNF role in order to be able to concentrate on solving the emergency while leaving the routine handling of the aircraft to the more junior pilot.

Pinger

Officially called an Underwater Locator Beacon (ULB). A piece of equipment attached to an aircraft's *Flight Data Recorder* (FDR) and *Cockpit Voice Recorder* (CVR). It is activated if the recorders are immersed in water and are used to locate the recorders in aircraft that have been lost at sea.

The pinger sends out an ultrasound signal that can be used to locate the recorder, but is only required by regulation to do so for 30 days. In practice this period can be longer depending on circumstances such as temperature.

The reason it uses sound and not radio signals is that radio signals are absorbed in water because water conducts electricity.

The signal does not contain any identification information, so the receipt of a pinger signal is not an indication of where it comes from. This can lead to signals from one thing being mistaken for something else.

Port and Starboard

On both aircraft and ships, port is the left side of a vessel when facing forward and starboard is the right side of a vessel when facing forward.

The use of port and starboard is traditional but is also clearer than left and right because those terms can get confusing as they depend on the direction the observer is facing. E.g. what's to someone's left is actually the right side of the vessel if that person is facing aft (towards the rear).

Pressurisation

As an aircraft climbs into the sky, the air pressure around it drops. At 8,000 feet, the pressure is about three quarters of the pressure on the surface, at 18,000 feet it is half, and at 36,000 feet less than one quarter. That's why aircraft cabins are pressurised so people on board can breathe normally.

The pressurisation comes from the surrounding, low pressure air which is being compressed by the engines. Most of that compressed air is used to burn fuel in the engine turbines, but a little of it is diverted into the cabin to keep it pressurised. (This air is called 'bleed air' because it is 'bled' off the engine compressor.)

The cabin is not kept at surface pressure but at around 8,000 feet altitude, or ¾ of the surface pressure. This is sufficient for normal breathing and saves weight because the aircraft fuselage can be built to withstand a lower pressure differential.

A rapid decompression of the cabin will be uncomfortable for people in it because the higher pressure in the body's cavities will escape rapidly. Ears will pop, some people get nosebleeds etc. But it is no worse than if a diver ascends too quickly from about 25 feet to the surface. Unpleasant, but it won't kill you.

A slow decompression is hardly noticeable, and as the air gets thinner and thinner, there is no fighting for breath or struggle for survival. The gasping for air associated with strangulation is not caused by a lack of oxygen but by an excess of carbon dioxide. The reason is not that people can't breathe *in* enough air but that they can't breathe *out* the CO_2 produced by their body's metabolism.

In high altitude asphyxiation, or hypoxia, there is no excess CO_2, because people can breathe out normally. Besides, with less oxygen, there is less CO_2, so no fighting for breath. Instead, the lack of oxygen leads to a pleasant euphoria which makes the person feel better and better. Not drunk, but absolutely on top of the world. Although enjoyable, this is dangerous because there is no feeling of anything wrong, so the person won't do anything about it, such as put on an oxygen mask. (This is why passengers are told to put on their own mask before they help others. If they wait, they will lose the awareness they need to put on their own mask.)

This lack of oxygen leads to loss of consciousness, and ultimately to death if oxygen supply is not restored in time. But it is probably one of the most pleasant ways to go you can think of.

Q-codes

These codes are relics from the days when radio communications were done in Morse code. Lengthy, but repetitive and standardised, questions and answers were given clear, specific codes to keep messages short and overcome language barriers. They all started with the letter Q (— — . —) to make them stand out.

A few examples:

QDM 'What is the magnetic bearing to your station' (question) or

'The magnetic bearing to me is…' (answer).

QFU 'What is the magnetic heading of the runway in use' (question) or

'The magnetic heading of the runway in use is …' (answer).

QFE The barometric pressure at a given geographic position, typically a runway.

QNH The barometric pressure at the mean sea level of a given region.

QNE Standard Pressure, or 1013.25 hPa (or mB), or 92.92 inches of mercury.

Q-codes are still used by amateur radio enthusiasts, but in aviation the last three codes shown above are the only ones now in common use. See *Altitude* for further explanations of the use of the various barometric pressure settings.

Radar

The word Radar is an acronym for **RA**dio **D**etection **A**nd **R**anging. Radar consists of an electronic signal being sent out from a rotating antenna. When the signal hits an object it is returned to the antenna again. The time it takes for the signal to travel to the object and back, together with the position of the rotating antenna at the time, show the position of the object that causes the reflection. This position is then shown on a screen as a 'radar blip.'

This so-called 'primary radar' is subject to a number of problems because the reflected signal is very weak. It can therefore be masked by electrical noise from various sources or weakened (attenuated) by things like large weather systems.

'Secondary Surveillance Radar' (SSR, often just called Secondary Radar) was introduced to solve these problems. It consists of equipment that sends out a radio signal at the same time, and in the same direction, as the primary radar signal. When this secondary signal is received by an aircraft's on-board *Transponder*, a signal is returned which is not only stronger than the primary return (and therefore less prone to noise and attenuation) but also contains data that positively identify the aircraft (the transponder code, called the 'squawk') and its altitude.

Civilian and military radar stations are completely separate and usually have no communication with each other. Civilian radar is used by *Air Traffic Control* to regulate the safe and orderly flow of civilian air traffic in *Controlled Airspace*. Civilian primary radar cannot determine the altitude of aircraft but relies entirely on secondary radar for altitude and positive identification in order to keep aircraft separated.

Military radar largely ignores civilian air traffic and concentrates on military aircraft. The military version of secondary radar is also different from the civilian system since enemy aircraft are unlikely to willingly identify themselves as such. A radar based 'Identification Friend or Foe' (IFF) system was developed for WWII aircraft, and various successors to that system are now in use.

Unlike civilian radar, military radar has some ability to measure the altitude of radar targets, but it is far less accurate than the civilian, transponder based, technology. However, as enemy aircraft are unlikely to volunteer their altitude, this is better than nothing.

SIDs and STARs

'Standard Instrument Departures' and 'Standard Terminal Arrival Routes' are details of routes and altitudes that have to be followed during departures and arrivals at large airports. They serve to ensure an orderly and predictable traffic flow in these busy areas.

Each procedure has a name, and instructing pilots to follow e.g. a 'Compton three golf' departure is a short and safe way of issuing a very long and complex set of instructions. The correct chart containing all the details of the procedure is then followed by the pilots.

Time: UTC and GMT

These abbreviations stand for 'Coordinated Universal Time' and 'Greenwich Mean Time.' In practice, on the surface of the Earth, they are the same.

The time of day or night is fundamentally determined by the position of the sun relative to your position on the Earth. When the sun is highest in the sky where you are (at its zenith), it is midday. The opposite position (its nadir) is at midnight, and everything in between is divided up into intervals we call hours, minutes and seconds.

The Earth makes one full revolution, 360 degrees, in 24 hours. The sun therefore appears to move across the surface of the Earth at a speed of 15 degrees per hour, from east to west. A given position, say 30 degrees east of another will therefore see the sun rise or set two hours earlier than the more westerly position.

For practical reasons, we deviate from this system and allocate the same time to large areas which strictly speaking have different solar times. Yet we put them in the same 'time zone' because it is convenient for a lot of other reasons.

But even with time zones, time still varies across the surface of the globe, and that gets very confusing when you move quickly from one zone to another, as aircraft do. For purposes of navigation and flight planning, pilots therefore refer to the time along the meridian that passes through Greenwich, just east of London.

This time is called Greenwich Mean Time ('mean' because actual solar time also varies with the time of year). When man began to move around in space, its definition was extended to include the entire Universe and renamed Universal Time Coordinated, but on the surface of the Earth, to all intents and purposes, the two are the same.

Why UTC you ask—it's not a perfect acronym. Well no, it's linguistic diplomacy. A compromise between the English 'Coordinated Universal Time' (CUT), and the French 'Temps Universel Coordonné' (TUC).

Top of Descent (TOD)

The point at which an aircraft must begin its descent from cruise altitude in order to follow a pre-planned descent profile. In general, the point is is determined by the distance to the destination and the altitude that needs to be lost, but it is also decided by things like restrictions on altitude and speed during the approach to the destination.

In this book, the TOD is determined by the distance the airliner is able to glide without engine power.

Transponder

A piece of radio equipment on board an aircraft that **trans**mits a res**pon**se when it receives a radio signal which is sent out by a *radar* station in parallel with the radar beam.

The transponder's signal is much stronger than the aircraft's natural reflection of the radar beam and is therefore better at locating the aircraft. The signal also contains details that positively identify the aircraft (the transponder code, or 'squawk') and altitude information.

Pilots normally set the squawk they are given by ATC so their aircraft appear on the controller's screen as expected. Other codes can be set to indicate unusual flight conditions such as radio failure, emergencies or highjacking.

There are other types of transponders than those used in aircraft. Submarines, for example, can use acoustic transponders which work with sound signals since radio waves cannot be used under water. These are not the same as pingers.

Trim

Primarily the nose-up or nose-down adjustment of an aircraft's horizontal stabiliser.

The horizontal part of an aircraft's tailplane consists of two parts; one fixed and one moving. The moving part is the elevator which is used to pitch the aircraft up and down to make it climb and descend.

The fixed part is called the horizontal stabiliser, and although it is 'fixed' in the sense that it does not move when the elevator moves, it can be moved by the aircraft's trim system. The horizontal stabiliser is adjusted according to the weight distribution (balance) of the aircraft so that the aircraft flies straight and level with the elevator in its neutral position.

A tail heavy aircraft will require the stabiliser to be trimmed to a more nose down position and vice versa.

Aircraft have separate trim systems for roll (aileron trim) and yaw (rudder, or vertical stabiliser, trim).

Waypoint

See description under *Airway*.

Weight and balance

The total weight of an aircraft consists of the aircraft empty weight plus passengers and crew plus baggage and freight plus fuel. That total cannot exceed a certain weight for takeoff, and many aircraft have a lower maximum weight for landing, taking into account the fuel burn en route.

The longitudinal distribution of these various weights also has to be carefully controlled in order to stay within certain limits. If these limits are exceeded, the aircraft will become too nose heavy or too tail heavy to be controlled by the *trim* system or the elevators (the vertical flight controls).

www.ingramcontent.com/pod-product-compliance
Lightning Source LLC
Chambersburg PA
CBHW071311250626
47159CB00004B/1388